# WADI

# WADI

A story to open the heart of humanity

**Aen Hussein**

Published by World Peace Press
in the United Kingdom

*— Dad —*

*I am dedicating this book to you
and the amazing man that you were
and always will be.
Thank you for encouraging me to be at the top.
I love you and thank you for loving me*

# Acknowledgements

To all who have contributed to the possibility of this book becoming a published work, I am very grateful to you for your words of guidance and encouragement.

To those who have contributed directly in helping me with various tasks throughout its lifetime this far, thank you and please accept this acknowledgement from my heart to your heart. They are:

- — Alison Mills
- — Gea S. Marinelli
- — Jane Hammett
- — Joan Collins
- — Julia Walker
- — Karl Pearsall
- — Kirsty McAndrew
- — Professor Kholoud Porter
- — Leila El Eryan
- — Maria Hampshire Carter
- — Rachel Elnaugh
- — Shareef Turner
- — Simon Horton

# Contents

# Preface

I started writing this book a few days after waking up one morning with a clear image and its story in my head. I was meant to write another book, and this is the one that came.

As the story unfolded, I had no idea how it would turn out and felt as if someone else was writing it. I cried many times as I read what I was writing, or realised what was going to happen next.

This book has felt like a gift to me and I am grateful for it. My intention is that, as you read, it will feel like a gift to you. It has helped me to feel peace deep inside my heart and to open it to many things that it felt closed to in the past. It has been healing me from the inside out and, in particular, in my relationship with my father, who died in 2003. May he rest in peace and awake in Heaven.

My intention for publishing this book is to be the cause of natural peace on this Earth in all our lifetimes and beyond. A natural peace is one that comes from and lives within each and every one of us. As war starts with a single intention that gathers others of the same intention, so too does peace.

*This above all: to thine own self be true,*
*And it must follow, as the night the day,*
*Thou canst not then be false to any man.*

WILLIAM SHAKESPEARE
POET AND PLAYWRIGHT 1564–1616

# Introduction

As I speak to people around the world about being an agent of peace, I get a lot of encouragement. When I then declare that my intention is peace in my lifetime, most people believe that this will not happen. Many feel that it's in our nature to be at war and that it's a normal, inevitable and even essential part of human survival.

I lived through the 1967 Arab–Israeli War. I was seven at the time, and was traumatised for years. I had the same nightmare for many nights. I am hiding in a ditch with my mother and sister; soldiers are jumping over us and don't notice us. Then the very last soldier does. He stops and fires at us; I am shot. Then I wake up.

I felt then that war was not normal and yet I too came to feel that it was inevitable. I now feel that war and the traumas it causes are wholly unnecessary and easily avoidable. I am passionate about creating the possibility that we will live in peace and have that be normal, inevitable and essential to our survival.

We human beings are eternal optimists; that's how we have survived this long and continue to break records. I am certainly an eternal optimist; I have faith in our humanity and feel that it's in our nature to be at peace. I feel that when we choose to feel peace on the inside, then peace on the outside will follow, and the world will be at peace.

I am inviting you to choose to feel peace on the inside – all the way inside – so that it's in all that you are feeling, being, communicating and doing. *I am inviting you to choose to have peace and have that be normal .*

You've always been there in my heart
and, once 1 started to let you go,
you set me free to be.

# CHAPTER ONE

# A First Time for Everything

Maya lived with her mother, who was very sad for a long time after her father died – Maya's father, that is. Maya could barely remember him; she was three years old when he died.

Maya's father was a tall man with dark brown curly hair and brown eyes. He was easy with himself and others. People liked him and he liked people. He had travelled all over the world helping to create fair-trade relationships and agreements between countries. His father had owned a small farm and had almost been squeezed out of business by sharp practices. Maya's father had grown up believing that everyone had an equal right to sell their produce in a fair market.

Maya's father had met Maya's mother at a party on his travels. It was a grand party at an embassy, with live music. The band had played the kind of music that you waltzed and had polite conversations to. After most people had gone home and the band had left, there were a few people sitting around the fire having a heated discussion about the latest economic hardships.

"Caused by years of government financial mismanagement," one man had said.

"It's no wonder we're in such a mess," a woman had commented. "No one really wants to govern these days; they just want to be popular so that they can stay forever."

Maya's mother had smiled, got up and sat at the piano and played. *This is the first day of the rest of my life*, Maya's father had thought as he watched her play.

Maya's mother was never one for politics; she wanted a quiet life. She would often quietly withdraw from conversations that she felt were going that way and act as if she had never been part of them. She preferred to play and listen to music. She had grown up with music all her life and both her mother and father were talented classical musicians who loved to perform. Maya's mother never played professionally, she preferred to play for her own enjoyment. She studied fashion design and, unlike her parents, managed to make a pretty good living.

Maya, her mother and father lived in a modest town house on the edge of town. It was simply furnished and decorated according to her mother's taste. Her mother had stopped working just before Maya was born and seemed happy enough being at home. She would occasionally take on private commissions to design a fantastic outfit for a past client. Maya's mother was always beautifully dressed and looked immaculate even when she was relaxing at home. Everyone thought Maya's mother looked beautiful, and Maya felt her mother looked sad.

Maya used to look forward to her father coming home from his travels because he would tell her all sorts of stories about people he had met, things he had done and places he had visited. Sometimes, when Maya listened to his stories, she would just look at him and watch his mouth move and listen to his voice. It gave her a warm feeling inside. Maya loved her father.

One day, Maya's father had come home feeling ill and went to lie down. Early the next morning an ambulance came and took him to hospital. Maya had stayed in her room and looked out of her window as she heard the sound of its heavy engine leave. Her mother had come to let her know that she needed to drop her off at nursery early so that she could go to the hospital to be with her father. Maya had simply got ready without saying a word; she was sad inside.

"Don't worry, darling," her mother had said. "He'll be fine. You know your father – he always is."

Maya hadn't known that her father would always be fine – and he wasn't. The next time she had seen him it wasn't him, it was his body. He had died.

Maya missed her father and the times they spent together. She felt sad and often cried. Sometimes she would forget to feel sad then she would feel bad that she had forgotten. At other times she would feel a sense of panic because she couldn't remember his face. Eventually those feelings only happened very occasionally and she would just cry, and cry, and cry, then feel okay again. Maya's mother didn't know how to be with all the crying, and only allowed herself to cry occasionally when she was on her own.

"There, there, darling," she would say in a sad voice that sounded far away, and Maya didn't understand why.

The day that Maya turned five years old, everything changed. Her mother seemed to wake up, as if from a long sleep. They had got back home from school and Maya had dashed upstairs to change into her party dress.

"You look the part, birthday girl," said her mother with a smile. "Now, let's do your hair."

Maya noticed the smile on her mother's face and smiled back; that hadn't happened for a long time. As she sat down at her dressing table and her mother stood behind her brushing her hair, she looked at her in the mirror. Her mother seemed different.

"Darling, you have beautiful hair, just like your father's."

"Did he have long hair as well, Mummy?"

"Not as long as yours. It was just as brown and just as curly, though."

Maya smiled. She liked that her hair was like her father's, "What colour were his eyes, Mummy?"

"They were brown too, darling," her mother replied and smiled back.

"Are mine brown?" Maya asked, opening them wide and looking at them in the mirror; she never knew what colour to call them.

"They are a kind of brown, I would say hazel – it's a light brown, and they're very beautiful."

Maya loved that her mother said her eyes were beautiful and she smiled, deep down inside. She remembered her father's eyes and how they used to shine.

"I loved Daddy's eyes," she said looking slightly tearful.

"And Daddy loved yours."

"I wish he would come back, Mummy." Maya had wanted to say that for a long time.

"I've been missing him too, darling, and this morning I chose not to and it's okay," replied her mother with a faint smile.

Maya's mother had chosen to smile and show her love again, and things became wonderful between them. From that day, Maya started remembering her father again; the things he said and did as well as what he looked like. It was as if her mother had made it okay again because she wasn't sad any more, and Maya did not like her mother feeling sad.

Soon after the party had ended and everyone had left, Maya put away her presents and got ready for bed.

"Darling, I have something amazing to show you. Get into bed and I'll be back in a short while," Maya's mother said with excitement in her voice.

Maya got into bed with pleasure. She liked going to bed anyway; she did a lot of her imagining there. She propped herself up with a pillow behind her back and waited. Maya's mother walked in with a colourful magazine and sat on the bed next to her. She opened it to an article on a page she had marked earlier by turning down the corner.

"Your father loved this magazine," she said, "and I haven't been able to bring myself to cancel or read it since he died. Today, I opened it and saw this." She pointed to a photo of what looked like bones on sand. "Look, darling," she said, "it's quite a story," and started reading.

The article in the magazine was about a remarkable chance discovery of a giant skeleton of a 'walking' whale. It had been found by an explorer a long time ago, along with several other skeletons of whales and many other sea creatures, in a valley in the Sahara Desert in Egypt. It was around one hundred and fifty kilometres south-west of Cairo, in the middle of a vast desert, miles away from any sea, and yet it had once been an ocean bed.

Maya looked at the photos, "Wow, I wish I'd discovered the skeletons, Mummy," then looked at her mother. "I'd like to be an explorer when I grow up."

"Would you, darling? Me too." Her mother looked at her and there was no response. Maya had started to daydream about being an explorer when she grew up, although she wasn't sure how you got to be one.

"Mummy, do you remember the whale that Daddy bought me?"

"I do."

"He told me that they were something else, not fish, and that some of them walk."

"Yes, I think you mean mammals."

"Well, when I took it to school to show in class, the teacher said that whales didn't walk."

Her mother smiled, she could tell where this was going. "Well, it seems that they do, or at least, they once did, a very long time ago."

Maya was imagining whales walking around on the sand with their tails up and waggling them around like dogs. She wondered how they'd got there and if they had got lost. After a few minutes of silence, Maya's mother read on. The valley, called Wadi El-Hitan, meaning valley of the whales, had many skeletons of what were giant whales that still had hind limbs. Although these limbs, complete with feet and toes, were too small to carry the weight of the whales – which could be as much as nine tonnes – it was at first thought to be evidence that their ancestors had walked on land.

"Mummy, how did they get there?" asked Maya.

"It used to be a sea many thousands of years ago, then it dried up."

Maya was upset at the thought of the whales being left behind when the sea had dried, and it seemed odd to her that they hadn't swum away.

"As it dried up," her mother continued, "it left all the whales and lots of other sea creatures trapped and now there's just desert and lots of skeletons."

The article went on to say that Wadi El-Hitan had now been declared a UNESCO World Heritage site, which meant it would be 'protected'. Maya wondered what it was being protected from.

"Mummy, why do they need to protect it?"

"That's a good question, darling. I guess it's to make sure that the skeletons are looked after so that lots of people can get to see them."

Maya wondered how you looked after a skeleton. It seemed a bit odd to her. She didn't bother asking though.

"Maybe it's also to make sure that no one can steal any of them," continued her mother.

Normally Maya would have thought that to be very funny, and have imagined someone wearing a whale skeleton and tiptoeing off with it through the desert in the dead of night. This time she didn't; she wanted to see them, so she was glad that they were being protected.

"Can we go see them after school tomorrow, please?" asked Maya excitedly.

"It's a long way, darling," replied her mother. "It's in another country."

"How far away is that?"

"Ooh, I'm not sure. A few thousand miles."

"And how long does it take to get there?"

Maya's mother put down the magazine, "You're serious about being an explorer then?"

Maya smiled back and nodded excitedly.

Her mother was quiet for a short while. "Darling, I would love to take you when you're older," she said finally.

"Like when I'm six, Mummy?"

"I think a bit older than that," replied her mother. "I'll also need to save up lots of money."

Maya was disappointed. She didn't know why her mother needed to save lots of money and could see that she was sad, so chose not to ask anything else for now and snuggled into bed.

As Maya's mother tucked her in, she leant over, gave her a kiss and stroked her hair. "It might take me a long time. I'll see if I can make it possible."

Maya did her best not to annoy her mother by asking all the time if she'd made it possible yet. It was hard, because she longed to see the whale skeletons. They were in her imagination a lot and reminded her of when her father had brought her back a toy whale from one of his trips to Japan. They spent a long time talking about whales and how they were not fish, even though they swam. She had named the toy Kiriyu and used to always make it walk even though she knew that her teacher was right – that whales swam. The thought of seeing the evidence that she might also have been right about whales walking, though, made it even harder. She did however manage to only ask her mother about it two or three times a week.

One morning, on a school holiday, she noticed that her mother had cleaned her bookshelf. She had moved her books around so that Maya could see the book that she had written her first story in. She leant over and picked it up and kissed it as if she was kissing her father, who had been the reason she had written it. She was only three at the time and he had come in, as he often did, to read her a bedtime story. He had sat on a chair by her bed and asked her which book she would like him to read to her.

"I'd like to hear one of your stories, Daddy," she replied.

"How about we hear one of yours instead?" he had asked.

She had thought for a while and replied that she didn't think that they were as good as his.

"Ah," he said, "let's see. Tell me something that's in your imagination right now."

That night she had created her first story. It was about how her toys waited until she was asleep and then played together, and how one night she pretended to be sleeping, and caught them out, then she had a great time playing with them the rest of the night.

The next morning her father had suggested that she make some drawings about her story and, when he got back that evening, he helped her create her first book. He bought her two scrapbooks and wrote out her story inside one of them. They then glued her drawings onto the blank pages he had left in between the writing. She had loved every minute of it and was looking forward to creating her next one.

As Maya remembered this, she realised for the first time that she had not written a book since her father had died. She picked up the second scrapbook and a pencil and started writing: *My book about walking whales and other sea creatures.*

Over the years that followed, Maya wrote many stories in that book. One particular story was her favourite. It was about a giant 'walking' whale called Kiriyu.

Maya illustrating her first book

Kiriyu was the head of a school of whales that lived in the Imogin Sea off the west coast of Africa. They were different from most whales and had large bodies, legs and feet, as well as very long tails. Even though all the whales at that time had legs and feet, they hadn't lost them yet, most were content to stay in the sea. There was plenty of food and fun to be had there.

"Why bother to do anything else?" they would say.

Kiriyu loved to do new things, explore new places, and create new homes for his 'tribe'; he liked that word better than the word 'school', and was encouraged in his new adventures by his mother, Malika. Although Malika was older and perhaps in many ways wiser, she was happy for him to take the lead after his father had died. He was a natural leader.

Kiriyu loved to learn, and he learnt things very quickly. One day, he decided that he would venture onto dry land for a new adventure; his mother had taught him to use his legs and feet, just in case they ever needed to live there as their ancestors had. As far as he knew, no other whales in his tribe had done this before and he shared his intention with his mother as he felt that there might be some danger. When he told her, although she was scared for his safety, as mothers often are, she felt that it was the right thing for a leader to do.

Malika helped Kiriyu make his plans and, when the day came, she told him that she loved him and that she had always known that he was a very special whale. She also told him that she knew that one day he would make this journey, and wished him well.

Malika was a wise whale and knew many things; she told Kiriyu of old passages under the sea that led to dry land and a desert in the east. She'd been told by her husband that these lands had once been part of the sea and would eventually return to it. She told Kiriyu that she didn't know how true this was and, that as far as she knew, her husband had never been there. Sometimes truth and imagination mix together to create stories, and it is difficult to tell which is which.

Malika also told Kiriyu that she knew of a fish that could help him stay alive for a very long time without eating. She told him where to look for this fish and that he had to swallow it whole. Malika said that, although this might seem strange, he needed to do it so that the fish could look after his tummy when he didn't have anything to eat. Malika also told him that he could only swallow the fish with its permission. This meant that he would first have to find it and ask it to come with him on his adventure into the desert, then it would have to agree to being swallowed whole. Kiriyu thought that it was a very strange story and that it might only be her imagination. However, he agreed anyway; he was a wise whale too.

As Malika said goodbye to Kiriyu, she had two tears in her eyes, one of sadness that he was leaving and one of joy that he was being Kiriyu – all a brave and loving mother could want.

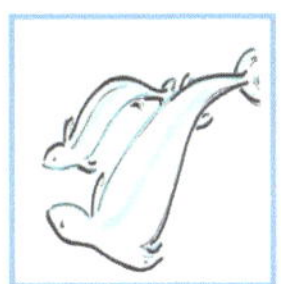

Maya's stories were filled with a magical mixture of imagination and reality, and her toys featured in most of them. As she grew up, they reflected the changing map of her imaginings and became more about things she would like to see and do, and people she would like to meet and be. Her drawings became beautiful colour illustrations and paintings. By the time she was thirteen, she had written and illustrated twenty-eight books.

# CHAPTER TWO

# A Dream Comes True

Maya had not been called Maya when she was born; this was the name that she had chosen for herself following a remarkable event, soon after her thirteenth birthday. Her mother had a surprise lined up as a birthday present; they were going to Egypt to see the whale skeletons in Wadi El-Hitan, the Valley of the Whales.

Maya had been waiting for eight whole years, and not always patiently. She knew that her mother, just like her father, rarely said that she might do something and never get round to it. She loved that they liked to make things possible even when they seemed difficult, and she had learnt to do the same. Maya had been out with her friends that evening after school, celebrating her birthday, and got back late.

"I know it's late, darling," her mother said. "Please come back down after you've had your shower and you're ready for bed."

Maya walked up the stairs thinking about her father and what he might have done had he been there. Even though she had stopped wishing every day that he would come back, she did wish that he would on her birthdays. She loved him very much and, in many ways, he was still very much alive to her. He was alive to her when she wrote her books, and particularly when she illustrated them, as he had encouraged her to. He seemed to know how to teach Maya to do things in a way that was easy and fun for her. She'd often wished he would stay at home and be her teacher.

Maya got ready for bed, came back down and sat next to her mother. "Mum," she said, "I love you very much and I'm sorry that I don't always say so when I feel it."

"That's fine, darling," replied her mother, and Maya wondered if that's what she really meant. "I have a surprise for you."

Maya's mother handed over a small folder that she had labelled: *Our journey to the Wadi*. Maya's heart skipped a beat as she opened it to see an itinerary of their flights, hotel bookings and jeep transfer to Wadi El-Hitan. They were leaving at the end of the following week! She jumped up and showered her mother with kisses and, as she did so, caught her mother's hairclip. Maya watched as her mother's hair came tumbling down and, much to her surprise and delight, her mother got up and shook her head.

"It's about time I let my hair down," she said, in an unusually loud voice, and they laughed and laughed and laughed.

The next few days were filled with laughter and happiness, and both Maya and her mother wondered what had stopped them before. They became close and talked all the time. They planned for a trip of a lifetime and did lots of things together that they'd never done before. They went shopping for clothes and stayed out late at the weekend. They cooked and cleared up together. They ate ice cream till they couldn't get up any more and fell asleep on the sofa while watching their favourite films. They shared memories of the wonderful man who had been Maya's father and put up some photos of him.

One memory of her father Maya shared was the time she had made up the story that became her first book. She told her mother how he had encouraged her even though she had felt that she wouldn't be as good as him. She told her that he had also encouraged her to illustrate it and that they had done some drawings and paintings together. Maya brought out some sketches of his that her mother hadn't seen before.

Maya's mother drew a deep breath. "Wow, he was really good, wasn't he?" She shook her head. "I've never really appreciated his drawings before."

Maya pointed out one painting that he had made of the desert. "I rediscovered this just yesterday," she said. "I was getting my things ready last night and I wondered about using it for the cover of my next book. Do you think that would be okay, even though I didn't draw it?"

"Of course," her mother replied. "People do that all the time, usually with the artist's permission, and I think we can assume that this artist would happily have given you his permission."

Maya smiled as she thought of her father being happy to give her permission to use his painting. She loved the way he had mixed the paints unevenly to create an irregular texture. She ran her hand over it. Maya loved feeling as well as looking at his art.

"Feeling is so important when it comes to drawing or illustrating something," he would say. "It's all about feeling." Maya was just beginning to understand what he meant.

Finally, the day they were setting off on their adventure came, and Maya had packed a little yellow bag that her father had bought her. Yellow used to be her favourite colour; it wasn't any more, not now that she was grown up. *It's okay*, she said to herself and chose to take it all the same, as it reminded her of him. She wanted him to come on their adventure and see how happy they were. *Perhaps he will somehow*, she thought and smiled.

She packed her favourite pens and pencils, especially the coloured ones. She packed a new sketchpad that her mother had bought her and a little camera that she'd got from some of her friends for her birthday. Most importantly, she packed her writing book, the one that had the story in about Kiriyu, the whale, and his adventures in the desert.

Maya looked at her book; she had all the drawings and painting that she had created since she was five in there. They were all tucked inside a sleeve that she had made from special wrapping paper. It was the paper from the last present that her father had given her. It may seem odd; she did still get presents from him. Oh, she knew that some were ones that her mother had bought because she felt that's what her father might have given her. At other times they would be things that Maya had found that she hadn't seen for a long time that reminded her of him, so she considered them to be presents from him. Other presents she got from him, which were the best ones of all, were memories that suddenly came to her. Although she was sometimes unsure that those memories were real, they were great presents because they were often a surprise, and she loved surprise presents.

Maya was pleased to be packed and ready early and as she went down the stairs to help make breakfast with her mother, she could smell something delicious before she got to the bottom.

"Mmmmm," Maya said as she breathed it in. "What is that belly-rumble-making smell?"

"It's fresh waffles," replied her mother. "I haven't made them for years and thought you might like something different for breakfast this morning."

Maya looked at the table, which was full of everything you could possibly eat for breakfast.

"Well," said her mother with a cheeky smile, "we may as well eat it all, darling; otherwise it will go to waste."

Maya didn't remember ever eating that much for breakfast before, and was surprised that she was that hungry.

"I don't know where you put it all!" her mother said, smiling. "I do love to see you enjoy your food, though, and you never know what you might get on the flight."

An hour and ten minutes later, the taxi had dropped them off at the airport and off they went through all the queues and all the beeping machines and out to the other side. They made their way to the gates where they could see the planes, and they were early; Maya's mother liked to be early. They found a great spot to do some plane-watching right by the glass where the planes were very close. Maya knelt on the chair and leant forward to get a closer look. She could see vans and trucks buzzing round the planes, preparing them for their journeys. She then started counting planes as they touched down and took off and noticed the different airline names and colours. She recognised some as country flags. Eventually her knees felt uncomfortable, so she turned around and looked at her mother.

"Do I have time to do some drawing?" she asked.

"Possibly, darling. I think we have another twenty minutes or so before they start boarding the plane."

Maya whiled away that time using her imagination, writing and drawing. She imagined she was a pilot and what her day would be like. She wrote a 'day in the life of Maya as a pilot' story. She loved to write; it came to her naturally and she wondered if she could do that for the rest of her life. She loved making up stories and she knew that it was partly because it reminded her of her father. After she had made up that first story about Suki, her toy bear, they would often make up a story at bedtime, rather than reading one from a book. Sometimes the stories would be really funny and not make much sense, which would make her laugh. Her father would make up one bit, then it would be her turn, and she would deliberately stop at a place that would make it hard for him to follow. He would then make a funny face, and that would make her laugh too.

Maya loved laughing before she went to sleep, even though her mother would sometimes ask them to stop. "How on earth are you ever going to get to sleep with all this going on?" she would ask with a smile on her face. "It's going to be pretty difficult to get to sleep after laughing so much." It never was difficult for Maya, though; it was a great way to get to sleep.

It was then time to board the plane and Maya let out a little yawn. She put away her things carefully and wished she was already there. After queuing at the gate and again to get onto the plane, Maya wondered where everyone else was going. There seemed to be so many people, and so many planes, going to so many places that it was difficult to imagine why. They finally found their way to their row and, after putting some things away in the overhead luggage compartment, she was very pleased to find out that she was sitting by a window. It may not have been everyone's ideal seat, as it was very close to the wing, which cut out quite a bit of her view; she was happy, though.

Maya settled into her seat and looked out at the wing. She could clearly see all the different pieces that made it work. She wondered which bit did what when the plane flew, and was looking forward to finding out. *I wonder how anyone ever thought of making a plane to fly in, or to make it of so many metal parts?* she asked herself.

"Darling, put your seatbelt on," said her mother, showing her how to.

The pilot then made an announcement introducing himself and giving out details of the flight path, timing and weather. He also requested that everybody pay careful attention to the safety procedures the crew were about to demonstrate, even if they had flown before. A very tall female crew member pointed to the emergency exits and showed them how to fasten and unfasten the seatbelts, use their life-jackets, get into the brace position, and leave the plane safely if they made an emergency landing. Maya looked at her and wanted to be that tall when she grew up. Then she smiled. *I must be pretty grown up already*, she thought. *That's why Mum's taking me to see the whales.*

Maya sat back ready for take-off and a bit of daydreaming. She looked around and once again the wing caught her eye; it made flying somehow real to her. She found herself wondering what the birds made of planes, giant flying things in the air that never flapped their wings. *It must be pretty weird for them*, she thought. *First, they're all out of proportion with other birds then, they don't have any feathers.*

She smiled to herself as she imagined a group of birds sitting on a fence having a discussion about a plane that had just flown by. "They don't flap their wings for a start, not even as they take off," said one bird, as it scratched its head. "They seem to fly in all sorts of directions, just going backwards and forwards, backwards and forwards," said another.

Maya was suddenly aware that the plane was speeding down the runway, and looked out at the wing again. She heard the engine noise change as it picked up speed and could see the runway underneath start to blur.

"Ready for take-off?" asked her mother.

Maya nodded her head excitedly as she felt a couple of bumps and the plane lifting off. "Woohoo!" she wanted to shout, and smiled instead, although flying wasn't quite how she imagined it would be. Then again, she couldn't think how she'd imagined it would be. *Funny how that happens. You haven't really thought about something and then, when it happens, it's not what you thought it would be. How does that happen?* she wondered to herself. Maya chose to park that thought, as just then she'd thought of another story about a bird called Oscar.

Oscar was a real whiz at figuring things out. He had heard about many birds being gobbled up alive by these giant flying things and wanted to figure out how to stop it from happening. It was pretty simple really, because he'd already worked out that the best thing to do was to steer clear of them.

He had noticed that when these flying things were in the air they didn't change direction much and so could easily be avoided. He put teams of scouting birds together and between them they soon knew which way these 'birds' flew – and when. Oscar had a feeling that they weren't really birds, and wasn't sure why, so he would sometimes go along with it because other birds insisted on calling them that.

Now armed with the flight routes and times, all they needed to do was let as many birds as possible know the details and that they should stay well away. Although this was a major task, it was really pretty simple as birds had a way of passing knowledge on to each other very quickly.

Oscar became a hero.

"What would you like to eat?" asked the stewardess, giving her two options. Maya chose the cheese sandwich. She didn't hear what the other option was and didn't like to ask, since she liked cheese anyway. She ate it quickly, as well as a bar of chocolate and a drink of orange juice. She tidied up her tray and stared out of the window again, where she could see the outline of a coast between the clouds below. *I wonder if there are people on the beach and swimming in the sea?* she thought as she let out a yawn and was soon fast asleep.

"Darling," said her mother, "Sorry to wake you. I thought you might want to look out as we're now flying over Egypt and will be landing in a few minutes."

"Yes," Maya said, stretching to wake herself. "Thanks." She had been dreaming a wonderful dream about swimming with Kiriyu. He was teaching her lots of skills that many humans had almost lost the ability to do. She learnt to dive and dart around objects and jump out of the sea and back in again. She learnt to breathe easily underwater and stay under for hours. She learnt to swim and stop quickly, then swim again, whenever she wanted to.

A few minutes later, they had landed. Maya had been waiting for such a long time to be there that she could barely wait to see the skeletons, maybe even Kiriyu, although she didn't like the thought of him as a skeleton. She was happy, she was excited, and she loved her mother for finding a way to make this trip possible.

"Thank you, Mum," she said, kissing her on the cheek.

Maya had often thought that she was getting too old to kiss her mother in public – not now, though! Maya smiled and kissed her mother on the cheek again; she was happy to be feeling close to her and was looking forward to spending time together.

They were met at the airport by their guide for the journey, Hassan. He was going to drop them off at their hotel and come back for them early the next morning with his jeep to set off for Wadi El-Hitan. They were going to drive through the desert, and what an amazing adventure it was going to be!

It was going to be a challenge to sleep that night, so after they had checked into their hotel and got ready for bed, Maya's mother brought out a scrapbook that she had put together especially for their trip. It was full of photocopies of magazine articles and photos of many of the discoveries that had been made in Wadi El-Hitan, and they sat in bed reading it together, eating popcorn that Maya's mother had packed. Maya loved this; she'd never eaten popcorn in bed before and it seemed all the tastier eating it with her mother.

Maya was surprised to learn that the first discovery of skeletons in Wadi El-Hitan was made as early as 1902, and that it had taken more than 100 years for it to become a UNESCO-protected World Heritage site. It was a major project with the government of Egypt, which was actually called the Arab Republic of Egypt. A buffer zone had been set up to protect the area and to create an open air museum. Simple paths and signage were made using natural materials. Buildings that housed visitor facilities were made from mud bricks so that they would blend into the surrounding scenery.

One of the articles read: *The construction of these facilities was made possible with the support of Gran Sasso National Park Italy, the government of Italy and IUCN, the International Union for Conservation of Nature.* Maya was impressed that people from different countries had helped each other to do this. She read about the many other marine fossils that had also been found in the area. There were fossils of molluscs, urchins, sharks, rays, crabs, turtles, crocodiles, sea snakes and fish. There were also sea grass and mangrove tree fossils, and Maya couldn't wait to see them all. This journey was one Maya had been on since she was five, or perhaps even before then, and here she was at last. Well, almost.

Maya had often dreamt about swimming with the whales, and she did so again that night. In her dream she was standing in the desert looking at the horizon and noticed how watery it seemed. She looked up at the sky and somehow she was underwater, and yet she could breathe as if she were above it. As she turned to see if anyone else was around, she felt herself lifting gently off the ground, which had become the seabed, and that's when she saw all the sea creatures.

They came out slowly from behind a pink rocky outcrop as if they had been waiting for her to notice them. She felt herself floating and twirling upwards as the sea creatures joined her. The water was sparkling around her and she could see the sun above and feel its warmth. She danced with the sea creatures as she allowed herself to float upwards in a gentle swirl. As she neared the surface, the whales joined them and she closed her eyes as one of them gently lifted her from underneath and took her to the surface. It was Kiriyu.

Maya's dream – swimming with Kiriyu

Maya's dream was remarkably vivid that night, perhaps because she was subconsciously aware of other remarkable events that had been happening in the world. There had been a number of earthquakes and earth tremors in the Far East that had caused some tsunamis; two in particular had been quite destructive. She had caught a glimpse of the devastation they had caused on the front of a newspaper someone was reading in the airport lounge, and she wondered what happens to sea creatures in a tsunami. She imagined that they would be fine and that they would save people who might otherwise drown.

Maya's mother had checked the news and the forecasts carefully. The flood-warning services had quite clearly shown the areas likely to be affected beyond the high-alert ones, and there was no indication that this would affect their journey. She had also checked with the travel agent, who explained to her that tsunamis only affected coastal areas and reassured her that this would not impinge on their journey.

Maya's mother remembered how destructive the last major tsunami in the Indian Ocean had been. It had happened the year before and affected many countries bordering the area and some well beyond. The trigger was an underwater earthquake that was the third largest ever recorded. The Earth vibrated with the impact and set off other tsunamis, including one on the east coast of Africa and another as far away as Alaska.

Maya's mother listened to the news before she slept that night. There had been agreement that the trigger for the first tsunami was an undersea rupture. This area had been assumed to be dormant, just like the one that had been the cause of the Indian Ocean tsunami the previous year. This undersea earthquake was small in comparison, yet it had been followed by an unusual number of aftershocks and a great deal of devastation.

There was much disagreement about the reasons why, and the same people who had voiced concerns about the human and economic choices that had contributed to the devastation of the Indian Ocean tsunami area were now protesting loudly. They cited the clearing of huge areas of coral reefs along the coast, to make way for fish and seafood 'farming', as one clear cause. Although they recognised the economic reasons for doing so, the danger of taking away this natural break was evidently a far more compelling one. No one had taken much notice of them then; now they were attracting public interest and concern was very high.

Maya's mother sighed as she switched off the news. "Thank heavens that we're going to be well inland."

The next morning Maya was woken up by the smell of breakfast. "Wow, room service!" she said. "Mum, you really have splashed out."

"Good morning, darling. Only the best on such a special trip."

Maya drank some freshly squeezed mango juice. "Deeeelicious! That's one of my all-time favourites!" she said, even though she'd never had it before, and they both laughed. She quickly ate a warm crusty croissant. "The rest of breakfast can wait." She wanted to have a shower and be ready in good time.

"Where are you going?" asked her mother. "You've hardly eaten anything."

"I'll eat after I shower, Mum. I want to be ready in time for Hassan."

Maya usually liked to daydream in the shower. Not today though; she was out quickly and put on some sunscreen and deodorant. She brushed her hair quickly and pulled it back off her face with her favourite hair band. She put on a new pair of shorts and a T-shirt that she'd had made especially for the trip; it had a picture of a whale on it. She topped it all off with a headscarf that she tied at the back; she'd read somewhere that it would keep the sand out of her hair. She looked at herself in the mirror. *Not bad*, she thought.

"Well, you look the part," said her mother as Maya came out of the bathroom.

"I know it's not quite explorer, Mum. I'm working on it though."

Her mother smiled. "Perhaps you could work on some more breakfast, then, while I'm getting ready?"

Maya ate a bowl of fresh fruit salad while she waited. She then ate some bread and cheese, wrapping some up in a napkin for the journey and putting it in her bag. She was ready to go.

Hassan was waiting for them in the lobby and greeted them with a big smile as they came out of the lift.

"Good morning," he said smiling. "It's a beautiful day, not too hot," he looked at his watch and smiled again. Hassan smiled a lot. "And you're exactly on time."

"Good morning," said Maya. "How long will it take us to get there?"

"Good morning," said her mother. "She's been waiting a long time for this trip."

"It'll take about three hours, maybe less," he replied and took their bags. "Follow me."

Hassan's jeep was by the front door and Maya felt like a princess as he opened the doors for them to get in. He put their bags in the back then handed them a bottle of water each; he'd brought a few in a cool box. He put the cool box on the front seat as they had both sat in the back.

"Just let me know when you want some more." He then made sure that they were comfortable and checked their seatbelts. "Can't be too careful," he said, and jumped into his seat in the front.

"You look happy," said Maya.

"I am! My wife found out yesterday that we're having our first baby, and I am very happy," he said patting his heart. He then set off with a screech of tyres.

"Woohoo, here we come!" said Maya out loud, and they all laughed. Hassan was a great driver and guide, pointing out lots of interesting places on the way, and stopping to pick up fresh watermelon and some odd-looking sticks similar to bamboo.

"Sugar cane," he said. "Best thing to get rid of thirst when you're out in the desert," and showed Maya how to get the juice out of it.

"Mmmm," said Maya. "It's delicious. Almost as delicious as the mango juice I had for breakfast. Thank you," And Hassan patted his heart, and nodded and smiled in acknowledgement.

Now out of the city suburbs and in the desert, Maya was in heaven watching all the sand dunes go by as the light of the sun threw shadows on them, creating many shades of yellow. *Perhaps it still is my favourite colour after all*, she thought. She asked Hassan what the word for yellow was in Arabic.

"*Asfar*," he replied.

"And what about the word for sand?" she asked.

"*Ramla*," he said. "Lots of *ramla*," and smiled as he made a sweeping gesture with one arm at the desert around them.

Maya liked that word and with that she was transported into her imagination with a tribe of desert people where she was Princess Ramla. She had always known she was a princess. Princess Ramla of Asfar.

Princess Ramla had a beautiful Arabian horse, a proud chestnut mare with a distinctive white mark on her forehead, and she called her Lula. Lula was good-natured, quick to learn and willing to please and, like her owner, was also high-spirited and alert. Princess Ramla could ride a camel just as well as anyone and, although they had distinct advantages over a horse on a long ride, she preferred a horse's temperament and ride. Besides, if you treat a horse with the respect and care it deserves, it manages well over long distances. The princess had been taught to ride by the king's horse trainer from a very young age, and many said that she could ride before she could walk. Although that was highly unlikely, Princess Ramla was certainly a natural, and a better rider than most of the king's horsemen.

Tours to Wadi El-Hitan usually went via the Faiyum Oasis then Lake Qarun, before reaching Wadi El-Hitan. Maya's mother had thought that this might be too much for Maya, since she'd been waiting for so long to see the whales, so they were going straight to the Wadi.

Maya looked very happy and was daydreaming as usual.

"Hassan's not the only one who looks happy," said her mother.

"I am happy, Mum. I've been dreaming about coming here for so long that I almost feel like I've been there already, and we haven't even got there yet!"

Her mother smiled; it was just the kind of thing her daughter would say. Her imagination always seemed to take her to places before she'd been to them. It was a gift, and her mother loved her all the more for it.

Maya looked in her bag and suddenly realised that she'd never read her story about Kiriyu to her mother. She pulled the book out very carefully to make sure that all her illustrations stayed in their sleeve.

"Mum," she said, "I'd like to read my story to you."

"A story about you?" her mother asked.

"No, a story about the whales that I wrote when I was five."

"Wow, really? I'd love to hear it."

They loosened their seatbelts slightly and wriggled around a bit to get closer together and Hassan smiled. Maya had to read quite loudly so that her mother could hear her over the sound of the engine and, as Maya read, they looked at the illustrations together.

"These are amazing, sweetheart. You did these when you were five?"

"It was because of Dad," said Maya. "He got me to start when I was three. I thought I wasn't very good then," Maya stroked the book. "Dad said I was, though, and I'm not sure what came first."

"What do you mean, what came first?"

"I mean, was I good and Dad saw it even though I didn't or … did I become good because Dad encouraged me?"

"That's a really good question," replied her mother. "I think you can be good, really good, at something if you practise and get lots of encouragement, and Dad was certainly good at giving people encouragement."

"I know," said Maya.

They were both quiet for a while, Maya remembering her father and Maya's mother remembering her husband.

"You know, it's different when you're encouraging someone with talent," said her mother. "It's there just waiting to be brought out, and you're very talented, darling. These," she said pointing at her illustrations, "take more than practice and encouragement."

Maya leant over and gave her mother a long hug and felt her mother's warmth. "I'm so glad I read the book to you, Mum."

"So am I, darling, so am I," Maya's mother replied, hugging her daughter a little tighter. "You should publish it. It's beautiful."

It was strange that Maya had never shared that story with her mother before; she had always associated her stories with her father and it had never struck her to share them with her mother. Maya was happy that she had done this before they had reached the Wadi, and the timing was perfect in ways that Maya was yet to realise.

When they finally arrived at Wadi El-Hitan, it seemed quiet. Maya had been expecting to see hundreds of people there. Hassan explained that most tours came here last on their journey, after they'd been to the Faiyum Oasis, Lake Qarun and the springs and waterfall in Wadi El-Rayan.

"Also," he said, "not a lot of people come here," and gave a slight shrug of his shoulders. Hassan then opened the back of the jeep and brought out a couple of cloths, "To protect you from the sun and the sand," he explained. "I'll show you how to put them on."

Maya wasn't too sure about putting one on, since she was already wearing a headscarf, then she chose to go along with it when she saw her mother putting on hers. "Could you show me again?" she asked Hassan.

"Sorry. Too fast the first time," he said, as he unwrapped the one he'd just put on and showed her again.

Once Maya was ready, Hassan explained that after he walked them round he had arranged for them to meet a very important man from the Egyptian Geological Survey team.

"His father was a very good friend of my father's; they went to school together," he smiled. "He is also very knowledgeable and will explain to you everything about the valley from ocean to desert."

Maya liked the idea of being able to ask questions of someone so knowledgeable. "Thank you, that's very kind of you." Right now, though, all she wanted to do was see the skeletons. "Let's get going, please. I can't wait to see the skeletons!"

As they walked around the paths looking at skeletons of unbelievably large whales, Maya wondered how these early whale ancestors walked around on land. She knew that they had once been land mammals that could also swim, and that eventually they had made the sea their permanent home. *Perhaps they had got too big to carry their own weight around?* she asked herself. *And so they chose to stay in the water; everything always feels lighter in the water.*

"The legs on these skeletons aren't big enough or strong enough to carry their weight," explained Hassan. "It's thought that they were used for other purposes, although we're not sure about those yet."

Maya was also wondering why this seabed had dried up, why there were so many skeletons here, and why more of the sea creatures hadn't just swum away. She was looking forward to meeting the man from the Egyptian Geological Survey team; she was sure he would tell her all she wanted to know.

After two hour's walking around, Maya wanted to sit for a while and asked her mother if they could take a little rest so that she could write down some questions.

"Yes, definitely. I thought you'd never ask!"

Hassan pointed towards one of the shelters and suggested that they rest there.

"That article was right," said Maya. "These shelters do blend in really well."

"You might want to see this skeleton first," said Hassan as he walked towards a very well-preserved skeleton … and that's when she saw it.

"Mum!" Maya shouted. "Come quickly," she said, beckoning her mother with her hands frantically. "It's Kiriyu, I recognise him!" Maya was so happy that she ran up to her mother to bring her over to show her.

"Do you think so, darling? They all look very alike."

"It's definitely him, Mum. I recognise the pattern of the rocks around him. And this dip right here – look, I'll show you."

Maya pulled out the scrapbook that her mother had made and pointed at a photograph in the article. "It's right here in the scrapbook, and this is the article you read me when I was five. Remember?"

Maya was so excited she felt she could almost fly.

"I think you're right. How clever you are, darling. Dad would have been so proud of you."

Maya couldn't imagine feeling happier than she was at that very moment. "He is, Mum, he is!" She had been circling around the skeleton excitedly as she spoke, and now walked back to her mother to hold her hand. That was also something Maya had once thought she was too old for. "Thank you for making this possible, Mum," she said. "Thank you."

Maya held her mother's hand and swung it backwards and forwards like a little girl as they walked towards the shelter.

Maya wasn't sure when the water came, it all happened so quickly. Everything had become very blurry and she didn't know if it was real or imaginary. She wanted to keep hold of her mother's hand and couldn't. She remembers letting go and floating off, and wondering if she might have fallen asleep.

Maya dreamt that Kiriyu came to save her and carried her on his back. It seemed to her like the most natural thing in the world, she'd done it often enough. She wondered if one of Kiriyu's tribe might have come for her mother, perhaps Malika, Kiriyu's mother. *Hassan*, she thought, *I hope they came for him too*.

Maya was sad in her dream; she thought all her sad dreams had finished when they stopped two years after her father had died. She thought she might be crying, and couldn't tell – there was so much water. *How can you tell if you're crying when there's so much water?* she wondered. She also wondered if her tears were making the water. So much water. This wasn't how she had imagined it would be.

Sometimes Maya would lie on Kiriyu's
back and look up at the sky

Maya was with Kiriyu and his tribe for some time; she didn't know how long, and there didn't seem to be a way of measuring it. Kiriyu taught Maya all he knew; how to breathe and feed herself while she was in the water, how to swim quickly then slowly, how to navigate effortlessly around things and be safe in the water. Kiriyu was also careful to teach Maya how to come up to the surface carefully. It may have seemed an easy thing to do; he knew, though, that it could be tricky. He also knew that although Maya had soon got used to being in the water for long periods, and didn't feel as if she needed to come up for air, she still needed to – it was important. Kiriyu would nudge Maya playfully upwards, then they would both come up for a while. Occasionally Maya would play around and dive down again and he would go after her. Although he could easily catch up with her, it was fun to pretend he couldn't for a while. Sometimes when they came up Maya would lie on Kiriyu's back and look up at the sky. "So much sky," she would say and breathe the air in deeply.

Kiriyu was a clever whale and a great leader. He took care of Maya and always made sure she had everything she needed; and he always seemed to know what she needed. He had a way of taking care of anyone and anything that needed taking care of, with no effort.

Kiriyu and Maya became very close, so what Kiriyu had in mind was going to be tough. Kiriyu chose the perfect day and nudged Maya to indicate to her to get on his back. He knew she didn't need to, he just liked her to. He told her that they were going on a very special adventure together, and off they went.

The water was particularly calm that day; it felt silky and rolled over Maya's body in a way that it had never done before. Everything felt different about today; she felt different and so did Kiriyu.

# CHAPTER THREE

# Ramla

When Maya woke up she was astounded by what she saw. She hadn't seen it for such a long time, not above water anyway, and there it was … sand. She could see that she was on a long stretch of beach and, now, that she was also slumped over something … an upturned boat? Maya had no idea where the boat had come from or how she'd got there. She had no idea how long she'd been there, or what had happened before that. She put out her hand and felt the sand. *Ramla*, she thought, and didn't know where the word had come from.

Maya pressed down with her hand and attempted to push herself up. She felt heavy. After a few attempts, she finally stood up and felt the sand under her feet; it felt odd. She felt odd too – older, although she didn't know older than what. She noticed her whole body was different; she was a woman. Her legs were long, sleek and strong, and her feet slender; she saw the sand and water swirling around them. *Maya*, she thought, and didn't know why.

As she looked around her, she could see that she was in a long sweeping sandy cove. "It's beautiful," she said, and was surprised at the sound of her own voice. She then wondered if she was on an island, or something much bigger. *Much bigger?* she quizzed as she realised that even something much bigger was still an island!

She sat on the sand and it felt good; she loved the way it caressed her feet and she loved its colour. She felt the sun on her back, warming her all over; it was as if it had never done that before.

Maya's thoughts drifted around with nothing to cling onto, as if nothing had happened to her before that very moment. Yet, something must have, because she wasn't expecting her body to look like it did, or her voice to sound like it did. *It doesn't matter,* she thought to herself. *All that matters is that I am here and here there is this, all of this,* she drew a deep breath, *and it's perfect.*

Maya fell into a deep sleep, deeper than she had ever slept before, and all the wounds of her past were healed. She dreamt of her father and how they used to read together and of the day he had died. She dreamt of her mother and of the last day she had held her hand in the desert. She dreamt of the desert and how it had become an ocean once more. She dreamt of the ocean and Kiriyu and knew that she could be with all of them whenever she chose. She felt lifted, as if she was being carried by gentle hands and laid down on a soft grassy bed. It felt good, it felt warm, and she felt warm and loved and loving, and knew that the past was behind her. All her sadness had been lifted away and she was safe and happy.

When Maya woke up the next morning, she found that she had been sleeping under a shelter in a boat which had been filled with exquisitely soft downy grass. She ran her hands over it and realised that she was wearing a garment made of a similar material. She couldn't remember how she came to be wearing it, or how she came by any of the things that she could now see around her.

*I think I remember the boat,* she thought, as she felt some connection to it. *And what about the shelter?* She looked around. *Someone else must have done this,* she told herself, looking for a sign. *Perhaps angels?* She was about to smile at that thought then wondered if she was dead or alive. *Is this Heaven?* she asked herself as she looked around again. *It's not how I'd imagined it*, and couldn't think what she'd imagined it would be like.

Maya lay still for a while and closed her eyes, as if to empty her mind to create a space to recollect something. Nothing came. She started feeling all over her body and laughed. *I must be alive, I can feel myself.* She then realised that she didn't know if that was true or not, although she did feel alive. She spent the next few minutes going backwards and forwards attempting to figure this out. *Okay, I can see myself and I can feel myself, so does that mean that I'm alive?* She couldn't bring any answers to mind and the more she dug for one, the less she felt she knew.

After a few minutes of lying there in silence, Maya wondered who built the shelter. *Well, if it wasn't angels, I guess I must have done*, she thought. Her thoughts wandered around and back to the subject of angels. *What are angels, and how do I know about them? Perhaps I'm dreaming?* And just then a woman walked in through the entrance, looking like an angel.

The woman, whom Maya later came to call Faye, was slender and had light brown hair, parts of which had been streaked a golden blonde by the sun. She moved with a lightness that gave her an angelic air.

Maya wasn't surprised to see Faye and smiled at her. Faye smiled back as she put a bowl of fruit down on a low table near the shelter's entrance and walked over to Maya. Her smile was amazing and she didn't so much walk as glide. The ground seemed to carry her, as if she belonged to it and it belonged to her. She handed Maya a drink as she nodded her head and smiled and went back to where she'd put down the bowl of fruit. She sat on the ground and Maya got up and sat down beside her so that they could eat together, as if this always happened.

Faye picked up a bowl that was already on the table and handed it to Maya. Maya put out both her hands to receive it as if it was the most precious thing she'd ever been given. As she looked at the bowl, she noticed that it was made of a light wood and it had the letter M on it. *M for Maya?* she wondered. *How could they have known?* Then she wondered who 'they' might be, since she had only seen this one woman.

Maya and Faye continued eating without saying a word. *Strange,* Maya thought, *I feel as if I've been here before and that I know this woman, yet I have no idea why.*

After Maya and Faye finished eating, Faye stood up, picked up the empty bowls and nodded at Maya, who duly got up and followed her out of the shelter … and there 'they' were! Several people, possibly angels, were walking around very quietly. They were mostly women, as far as Maya could make out. Then, a man stepped forward and presented her with a cloth, which had the letter M woven into it, and she knew that he had made it for her. She smiled and accepted it and felt that she was here to stay.

Faye led Maya to a bathing area and, with a nod and a smile, left her to it. She hadn't said a word, yet Maya somehow felt that she'd let her know exactly what to do. Maya felt a warm glow inside as the water touched her skin; she was happy in a way that she hadn't experienced before. Everything felt new to her, including herself, and it felt simple and easy. *That's the way it's meant to be…* she said to herself as she bathed, *…easy,* and chose to stop attempting to work out whether she was dead or alive.

When Maya had finished bathing, she dried herself with the cloth that the man had presented her with. It was a beautiful cloth, made of a fibre that was soft and absorbent and felt good against her skin. She reached out for the garment that she had been wearing earlier and found several more had been placed there for her to use. She picked out a pale yellow tunic and slipped it on, along with some long trousers that she tied at the waist.

Is this Heaven?

The cloth that the garments were made of was loosely woven, soft yet strong, and lighter than the cloth that the man had given to her earlier. She picked up her things and walked back to her shelter to put them away. She folded them and put them in a basket beside her bed, or boat, as it actually was, and placed her bathing cloth on the end to dry. As she did this, she noticed that the boat had been placed on a beautiful wooden plinth to keep it steady. *Those angels are pretty clever*, she chuckled to herself.

Maya walked out of her shelter and followed the path that she had seen Faye take earlier, past the bathing area into the trees and beyond. She looked back to see her shelter and noticed a sign near the top that had two words on it: "Maya" and "Kiriyu". Maya didn't remember telling anyone her name and wondered how anyone could have know it. She also didn't know who Kiriyu was although she felt she knew the name somehow. She looked around at the other shelters and noticed that none of the others had any names on. She walked on. *I'm not even going to attempt to make sense of that*, she thought. She felt light, happy and free, and that was everything she needed. Nothing else mattered

Beyond the trees there were many people tending to the land and plants, all sorts of plants bearing amazing fruits and grain. The fragrances mixed subtly and blended with the air naturally. She breathed the air and felt it passing through her nostrils, fresh and vibrant as if it had colours. To one side she noticed a group of people and, as she walked towards them, they made way for her, and there was her place, as if it had always been there, beside a woman in a pale green gown. The woman smiled and nodded at Maya as she showed her what she was doing.

The group were treating the stalks that were left over after grain had been stripped off them, to make them soft, supple and strong. Some were being stripped to make thinner fibres and others were being dyed with soft colours, mostly pale yellows, greens and browns. Maya was to lift out the fibres when she thought that the dye had taken enough, and hang them out to dry on special frames in the shade. She looked over at the ones already blowing in the breeze and loved the subtlety and gentleness of their colours.

Maya learnt quickly, as did everyone there, it seemed, and very soon she was making the dyes herself as well as creating new ones. She loved experimenting with different things to see what colours they would create. She also learnt how to make different dye patterns by curling, knotting and tying the fibres before she dyed them, and sometimes while they were drying.

Over time, Maya also found new ways of refining the dying and weaving processes, and became very proficient at making a new cloth that was very light and durable. It was also very flexible and was useful for filtering out impurities from drinking water. Maya made special gowns and tunics from it for everyone to wear on warmer nights. She painted a special little picture on each one, like an emblem, specifically for each person. Everyone loved them, especially the man who had presented Maya with the cloth the day that she had first walked out of her shelter. Maya chose to call him Kaiyo, since he seemed to have no name (few people on Ramla did), and the emblem she had painted for him was a whale. Kaiyo loved it, and the tunic that she had made him; he wanted to wear it always.

Maya started using the dyes along with some of the leftover liquid from boiling the stalks to make different paints. Boiling the liquid gently for longer made the colours 'sticky', and she could paint many things with them. She brought beautiful colours into the community and painted all sorts of things that people brought to her, mostly clothes, crockery and all sorts of wooden objects. Some of the crockery was made of a kind of baked mud and the paint didn't show up on them much; it just made light patterns, which everyone seemed to like.

Maya's creativity showed in everything she did; she found it easy to be creative. There was always time to be, to do, to connect and to create. Ramla, as she came to call this place, had a kind of easy magic, and things just *were*. The plants grew and gave in abundance, and the people, if indeed that's what they were, did everything with a sublime ease. Everyone on Ramla had a natural place and rarely spoke, yet everything was clear. Maya loved this. *It's just perfect*, she would think. *Words can sometimes get in the way of what you mean.*

Towards the end of the day everyone would gather to share food, smiles and laughter. New inventions and ideas would be drawn up and agreed, usually without any words being exchanged. People naturally took it in turns to take the lead, although one woman, known as Angel, often did, especially when any actions needed to be agreed. She was great at knowing exactly who had the skills to carry out a task well. People accepted whatever they were asked to do willingly and everything was done with a calm excellence.

Maya felt that Angel was like a queen rather than an angel; it seemed to her that she was queen of all she surveyed. She was bold, she was practical, she was wise and she was observant. She looked out for everyone and somehow held them together. Community and social values were important to her, and she was a natural leader. Maya painted a watchful bird as her emblem.

Kaiyo was also a natural leader and quite different from Angel. He was very skilled and taught people how to make things. It was he who had shown Maya how to make brushes to use for her delicate paintings. He seemed to execute both large and delicate tasks with great passion and skill, as if he was born to them. He said he never used to be like that. This was very interesting to Maya, as she had no memory of what she had been like before, and had assumed that everyone else was the same.

As Maya grew she and Kaiyo spent a lot of time together. Maya loved to watch Kaiyo make things, and acquired many skills and ideas through him. He passed on what he knew and helped people create new things naturally. Maya loved the way he connected with people; he seemed to be everyone's close friend. When he spoke it was inexplicably easy to hear him, and it hardly mattered what he said. He had a quiet strength that was easy to love and always seemed to be there whenever you needed him, as if he already knew.

Maya asked Kaiyo one evening how he knew what or how he had been before.

"I don't always know; it's just a feeling and other times it's a memory," he replied.

"How do you know it's a memory and not a dream?"

Kaiyo smiled. "I've never been much of a dreamer, so I assume it's a memory."

"That's just the thing," said Maya. "I am a dreamer, and I don't remember anything of how I was before."

Kaiyo looked at Maya and broke into a wide smile. "I think that's why you're so creative, Maya."

That was the first time she thought he'd ever said her name, and it sounded warm. "I feel I was always like that; I'm not sure though," she said.

"I feel you were too," he replied, and that was good enough for her.

It was somehow comforting to Maya to know something of what or how she was before she came to Ramla, even though being there was perfect as far as she was concerned.

Maya did have some knowledge of what had happened before she came to Ramla. She knew, for example, that she had come there with "the Waters", as they were referred to there. She knew that things were different before, and that something had caused the Waters to come. She also knew that, despite the fact that hardly anyone on Ramla talked about the Waters, they had created a new world, a world where everyone had their place, a world where everyone fitted in, a world where no one needed to speak to be heard or understood, a world where no one had to have a name. What Maya didn't know, yet, was that Ramla was different from anywhere else.

That night, Maya headed for Kaiyo's shelter and, as she approached, she knew that he wasn't alone; there was nothing unusual about that, since he was one of very few men on Ramla. Maya wanted to be with him – not in the way that things were on Ramla – so she chose to wait and trusted that she would know when the time was right. She had always felt a magical connection between them and, although it had gone unsaid for years, she knew that it would be said – just not now.

The year that the Waters came, Maya was thirteen. They came quietly and quickly, although the 'experts' had predicted otherwise. The experts had indicated that water levels would rise rapidly, and any flooding would be fairly localised and temporary. This was not the case and many 'amateurs', as the 'experts' liked to refer to anyone else, had predicted this. They had predicted that flooding would be far worse than the experts had indicated, in terms of both level and area; they also predicted that some flooding would take years to subside, and could remain permanently in some places. The experts had publicly ridiculed these predictions, insisting that they were highly unlikely, and that any effect on sea levels would be negligible.

"Negligible can be a dangerous word," said one amateur. "We're supposed to believe that we can ignore its effect. Ignoring the signs, and saying that they're 'negligible', is exactly how we got here. If there is one thing we can be sure of, it is that there are always consequences, and we cannot always be sure what they will be."

The minor tsunamis in the East that had been triggered by minor earthquakes, which at first seemed to follow a predictable pattern. People were happy that any flooding was 'localised', as the experts had predicted and, for a while, most of the world went on as if nothing had happened. The minor quakes were under the sea, near the area that had ruptured several years earlier, and the aftershocks had been felt, as expected, several hours later. Some seismic activity continued, however, which went unreported, and eventually a further rupture, accompanied by a sudden and near-catastrophic rise in sea temperature, occurred. This rise in temperature changed the course of established sea currents and water levels in many areas rose past any predicted levels. In less than three days, the map of the world was unrecognisable.

It was the first time in living memory that all wars had stopped. Many millions of people died in the floods, and those who survived had stopped counting. There was an eerie silence everywhere and most communication channels were down. Those that were still up went unused for some time, because people barely knew what to say or do.

Finally the eerie silence began to turn into a new way of life. For whatever reasons, the Earth had been pushed to the brink; it was emerging transformed. Many animals had died in the floods and people's diets had changed dramatically. There was an amazing proliferation of new and nutritious plants where the water had subsided. They provided food and basic materials from which to make shelter as well as fibre for cloth. Humanity connected with itself and its environment and was emerging out of the near-catastrophe with what would finally become a perfect peace.

When Maya eventually came to know something of what had happened, she felt that the world had been washed anew. People emerged with a new capacity for everything and everyone. Their hearts opened wide and their energy became clear, generous and receptive. Maya saw this energy in beautiful radiant, warm and gentle colours and it was easy to know how everyone was.

Many years had passed and Maya was happy on Ramla. Yet, every so often she would feel that there was something missing and wonder if anyone else felt the same. She wondered if the missing thing was what had happened to her before she came to be there. Hardly anyone talked about what had happened to them before, mostly because they didn't remember. She knew, though, that some people did, like Angel and Kaiyo. Kaiyo didn't remember much. "Just feelings," he would say, and she knew that feelings mattered.

Maya did remember some things, like the day she woke up on her grassy bed in her shelter; she remembered that she had thought that angels had made it. *How did I know about angels?* she would ask herself. *I must have remembered that from another time.*

Maya would sometimes muse and daydream, especially when she was inventing or creating things. She would occasionally ask people what they felt, mostly Angel and Kaiyo, as she never got much of an answer from anyone else. Others would just smile, look pensive for a second or two, and then shrug their shoulders when nothing came to them.

Then, one morning, Maya woke up with a yearning for the 'sea'; she had remembered that this is what it was called before the Waters came. She hadn't been in it since the day she came to Ramla and didn't know why. She wondered if there were other lands like Ramla and if anyone had been to explore them. After completing her work that day, she asked Kaiyo. He looked at her, smiled and beckoned her to follow him. Kaiyo took Maya through the woods and out into a small bay that she didn't remember seeing before. She was delighted to see a boat, and Kaiyo explained to her that a few of them had been building it for a while.

"That's strange," she said. "No one's ever mentioned it."

"Maybe no one thought we'd actually ever use it," he replied. "Everyone's happy to be as they are."

"Me too," said Maya. "Surely not forever, though?"

They sat together for a while looking out at the sea. "Besides," Maya said suddenly, "why build a boat if you've no intention of using it? There must have been some intention."

Kaiyo smiled. "Somehow, I knew the day you came to us that we'd have this conversation."

"So, why not mention it before? I mean, look at it!" she replied as she got up. She stood looking at the boat for a while; it was small and sturdy. She put out her hand to feel the wood. "It's beautifully built." She took a deep breath as she walked around touching the boat. "Surely it deserves to be used on the water?"

"It was Angel who suggested we build it," he said. "She was the first one to know and asked me only two days ago if you'd ever brought up the subject."

"She did? Well, let's go and talk to her then, and let her know that I asked."

Angel suggested that they call a meeting straight away and that Maya take the lead. A few minutes later Maya stood, tall and magnificent, to address everyone. She was graceful, gracious and commanding, and everyone listened to her.

"I feel that there are other lands out there, other life and other people," she said. "I feel them in my heart."

"We feel them too, we just don't know how far away they are, though," said the woman who had taught Maya how to weave her fibres into cloth.

"I understand," said Maya. "It could be a long way away, or—" she pointed to her right, "it could be on this very same land in another direction." She looked around. "Who knows? Has anyone been to find out?"

Everyone fell silent. Then, as Maya saw Angel smile at her, she continued, "We all came out of an amazing event, and we feel that others did too. It had never even occurred to me before this morning. And that boat you've built is beautiful," she smiled. "When I saw it, I felt your intention, so how about we complete on that intention?"

Maya's question changed the group dynamics and a few people started to respond. Angel smiled a soft wide smile and Maya felt it in a way she hadn't felt before.

"It would be great to find out," Maya heard someone say.

"Imagine how many more skills and inventions we might find," another voice said.

"It would be amazing to meet new people," said one woman who then stood up, and that changed the dynamics again.

"They may not be like us," said a young man.

"Yes, they may not," agreed Maya. "There are no guarantees, just adventure."

Maya felt interest rise and people started to stand up and make comments.

"If they'd had intentions that weren't good, they'd have been here by now, and I for one am curious," said one woman. "I'd love to go with you, Maya."

Maya felt her heart expand. *At last*, she thought, and smiled at the woman in acknowledgement. She then walked over to her and said, "Well, that makes two of us at least."

This raised some laughter, and Maya sensed it was nervousness. "Perhaps we can have two adventures?" she continued. "One on land and one by sea. I know there's a lot of water out there, and I haven't ventured near it since I came here." Maya felt some relief in the crowd at those words. "Does anyone have any ideas of the most likely direction for other land?" she asked, and a few people came forward.

Kaiyo cleared an area on the ground to make a drawing as others came to help. "Right," he said. "Where do we feel other land might be?"

People crouched down for about an hour, exchanging feelings and ideas, and came up with a makeshift map. Maya then sketched it out on a piece of her special cloth so she could make a painting of it the next day; she wanted to make sure it would last. She was excited.

Maya stood up again and thanked everyone for their help. "So," she continued, "who else would like to join us?" And, before she could look round, Kaiyo was standing at her side.

Kaiyo smiled as he always did and she smiled back; he was always there whenever she needed him. He then placed one hand on Maya's shoulder and everyone knew that this signalled his readiness for a union. Maya smiled and understood straight away, even though it was the first time she had been aware of this signal. It was a very unusual happening in Ramla, given that there were so few men there. She placed her hand on his, indicating her agreement, and so it began.

That night, many people came to Maya's shelter bringing her gifts and words of support. Several more volunteers came forward, including the woman who had first spoken up in the crowd. This made a team of six, as many as the boat was built to take.

Kaiyo was the last to come to Maya's shelter that night and, as they spoke, something else happened that they had both dreamt would happen one day. Their words, their feelings and their senses merged and, as their bodies merged too, it was sensual, sensitive and sublime.

The next morning Maya woke up to find that Kaiyo had laid out a breakfast feast. They ate almost without taking their eyes off each other, and smiled. Once they'd eaten, Kaiyo took Maya by the hand and led her back to the boat; he had painted the words *New Explorer* on the side. Maya smiled a deep smile and felt an energy that came from somewhere beyond her.

Kaiyo had prepared for a long trip. He had gathered enough provisions for a six-month sail. They consisted mostly of dried fruit and pre-cooked dried grain so that they would be as light as possible. He was also making a special water filter using Maya's cloth.

"Great idea," said Maya as she climbed on board.

Kaiyo had been spending much of his time getting the boat ready and said that it could be ready as early as tomorrow.

As Maya stood on the deck, she opened her arms wide, twirled around and felt the wind in her hair. She looked up at the sky in gratitude and opened her mouth wide. "I'm ready now!" she shouted, and turned back, looked at Kaiyo and smiled. "We need to be sure that the others are ready too, though."

Kaiyo smiled back. "They'll be ready soon enough."

Once Kaiyo had completed the onboard preparations, the team of six explorers got together regularly to take the boat out for trial sails. They worked in harmony to navigate and steer. The boat handled well and Kaiyo was a great captain. Everyone took their places naturally and carried out tasks with their usual calm excellence. A week later they were ready to go.

Maya wanted Faye to come with them on their journey, and was sure that she would steer them to land easily. She also knew that Faye needed to stay in Ramla and, throughout the week, Maya went to her to learn from her connection with the land.

Faye smiled when Maya first approached her that week. "We need to talk," she said.

"We do," replied Maya in agreement. "Faye, I would love you to come with us."

"I will be with you in many ways, Maya – as well as here tending to the land."

Maya looked at Faye as she helped her to fix frames for new fruit trees to climb up. "Yes, I understand," replied Maya, and watched Faye as she tied the branches and gently curled the tendrils around the frames.

"Now, put on this blindfold and let your senses lead you," said Faye. Maya bent down and Faye tied a cloth around her eyes. "This will help you connect with the land," she said.

Maya felt transported into a different world. "Will I have to wear it all the time?" Maya joked.

"In a way," replied Faye. "Sometimes we have to close our eyes to truly see."

Maya became fully present in that moment; her senses heightened and she smelt the air. "It's magical."

"You learn quickly, Maya; you have trust in your senses."

"That's the magic of Ramla," replied Maya.

"Yes, that's true. There is a sense of freedom here that creates that magical space. It is clear, though, that we all have different areas in which our senses are particularly sharp."

Maya's senses were sharp in many areas: they were particularly so when it came to people. She knew, for example, when someone was approaching her, whether it was a man or a woman; she didn't need to look. She also knew their feelings and could make almost instant images of them. She could feel people's intentions and see their energy in colours.

"Let's begin," said Faye as she took Maya by the hand and led her around. "Now, what can you sense?"

Maya picked out several things she sensed as she walked around. "Freshly cut wood, a breeze from my right, dry sandy earth, moisture, seeds in the air, and the scent of new buds," she said. "A rustling in the plant straight ahead, the smell of dry grass—"

"What kind of grass?" asked Faye.

"The kind that we've just been using to tie back the plants with."

"How can you tell if it's dry and not still growing?"

"It has a slightly powdery, dusty smell."

"Great, and what about this one?" asked Faye.

"That's been boiled recently; it has a sweet, damp smell."

Maya spent an hour with Faye that first time, feeling, smelling, touching and sensing. She learnt quickly and began to distinguish between different kinds of soils and would know if it was good for growing plants. She learnt to sense if she was near fresh or salty water. She learnt to sense the air around her and its changes.

Faye loved teaching Maya, and they spent many hours over the next few days connecting with her deepest senses and instincts. Faye transported her into a new level of being for all her journeys to come.

By the time Maya got back to her shelter each night, it was dark and most people were inside their own shelters. On the last night there was a bright, clear new moon and Maya knew that the timing was perfect. Kaiyo wasn't at her shelter that night; he'd been sharing most of his time between the boat and his shelter preparing for their adventure. As she cleaned her teeth, she smiled at the brush that he had made her out of a fibrous stalk. She put on a fresh gown and smiled as she ran her hands over it. She smiled at everything she saw, felt and did, especially as she eventually lay on her bed, the one that Kaiyo had made her from her boat. *It's time to sail away*, she thought, and fell into a beautiful sleep, the kind of sleep that every explorer should have before they set off on an adventure.

Maya dreamt of faraway lands and people. She dreamt of Faye guiding her to them and to new discoveries beyond them. She dreamt of beautiful butterflies with magnificent wings. She dreamt of dancing in a forest with children with the butterflies all around them.

There had been no children on Ramla until the day that Maya had come ashore, and she hadn't known how old she was then.

She had always had a childlike innocence that enchanted everyone and everything, and that showed in everything she was. Although she didn't know it, she was almost nineteen, and it was going to be quite a year for Maya, and for Kaiyo. It would be a year full of new adventures and discoveries, the biggest one of which would be having a child.

Maya's dream that night was a revelation and was filled with many things that would come to be. She was awake early the next morning and, as she opened her eyes, she looked around to check if she was on the boat or on land. Her dream had been so vivid that she felt she knew exactly where the land that she had dreamt of was. It was to the east, where the sun came up in the morning, and yet, the night before, they had planned to sail west, away from the morning sun. She ate some fruit, picked up a bag that she'd prepared a few days earlier, and hurried down to Kaiyo's shelter. She wanted to tell him about her dream and that they needed to sail east.

Kaiyo wasn't at his shelter, so she ran down to the beach. She got into one of the rafts and rowed out to the bay where the boat was now moored.

Maya's heart filled as she approached and saw Kaiyo. "You were up early," she shouted, as he threw down a rope.

"Actually, I slept on board. A few last-minute preparations."

"Okay," she said throwing her bag up, and climbed the ladder. Kaiyo reached out with his arm and Maya held on to it at the elbow, as he'd taught her to. She felt an amazing strength and energy as she held on to him and he helped her on board.

She looked around and smiled. "This is it," she said, and then said it louder. "This is it!" She twirled around as she had done the first time she'd been on the boat.

Kaiyo smiled and grabbed her hand as she twirled around. "Just wait till you see this," and led her below deck.

"Wow," she exclaimed in delight as she looked around. "You've been busy!"

Kaiyo had put up many of the paintings that Maya had made for him throughout her time on Ramla. They were mostly on clothes that she'd made for him and some were on pots; he'd somehow managed to put them all up on the wall. She smiled and stood back to look at them; they seemed to tell a story. It was a story of a young girl growing up among a group of whales; one whale in particular featured in many of the paintings and had a distinctive white marking on its forehead.

"I've never looked at them quite like that before. I painted these at totally different times, I mean; they weren't in a sequence."

Kaiyo nodded. "Yes, I know."

Maya scrunched her eyes slightly as she took a closer look. "They were random images – at least I thought they were when I was painting them."

"Yes, I know," repeated Kaiyo. "I thought so too until I was putting my things together yesterday, and then I saw this sequence."

"Hmmm, do you think the little girl is me?"

"I do."

Maya was silent for a few moments; she was wondering how much of those images were imagination and how much memories. "Thank you, Kaiyo," she said. "I love it that you did that, and I love you."

Kaiyo gently pulled her towards him and whispered slowly, "And I have always loved you, Maya."

Seconds later, they heard the sound of cheering, and the others climbing on board, "This definitely is it," said Kaiyo as the others came below deck to join them.

"Everyone's up so early!" said Maya.

"We can barely wait," said one.

"We're looking forward to you guiding us to new lands," said another.

"Ah," she said, "that reminds me—"

"We're heading east," they all said and Maya looked at Kaiyo.

"I let them know that we're heading east as soon as you let me know," he said.

Maya knew that she hadn't told Kaiyo about her dream and loved that he knew without words. She was also happy that everyone knew too and that they were happy to be guided by her.

"Let's get going, then," she said, and they all made their way back above deck.

It was a clear, calm and bright morning, and many people had gathered on the beach to see off the small group of explorers. They waved at them enthusiastically and as Maya waved back she felt that many more would have liked to come with them.

Faye and Angel came alongside in a raft; she'd never seen either of them anywhere near the water before, much less *on* it.

"Have a great adventure," shouted Angel. "You carry all our hearts with you, Maya. You've given us a new energy and feel for life that's as beautiful and boundless as you are."

Maya thought that she'd heard a tremble in Angel's voice as her words carried in the wind.

"Maya," said Faye, "you've left a mark on Ramla that has inspired many people to go exploring on land, and we want to thank you. You never know, we may even take to the water and come out to find you one day. Enjoy your grand adventure."

As they rowed away, Maya heard Angel's voice again. "Thank you!" she shouted. "Thank you, all of you. We love you all, and may all the angels be with you." And, in that instant, Maya knew that Angel was an angel.

∽◎ CHAPTER FOUR ◎∽

# Healing Waters

The group of adventurers headed east and within thirty minutes they were out on the open sea. It was relatively calm and the boat seemed to know exactly where it was going. They were all happy in each other's company and looked out for each other. In between looking after the boat and preparing and eating simple meals, there was much sharing and laughter.

"I feel so energised and alive," said one of the women, who had become known as Nala. She was the one who had taught Maya to weave. "I am loving being out here, I feel I can breathe."

Nala had never contemplated being on the Waters before; she had felt no connection with them and had no recollection of how she got to Ramla. She loved being part of the small community on the boat and seemed different every day, becoming animated and alive.

There was another man in the group, other than Kaiyo, that is. He had not spoken up the night Maya had addressed everyone. He had helped create the makeshift map and felt no inclination at the time to go with them. The next morning, though, he felt differently and went to talk to Angel. He told her he felt he could be a valuable part of the group, although he wasn't sure how. He was one of only a few men on Ramla and wanted to be sure that the community would be happy for him to go.

"I appreciate you coming to talk to me," said Angel, "and I feel sure that everyone here would be happy for you to join the group, as would the group."

He smiled and nodded in appreciation. "Thank you, Angel, I appreciate your support. I'll go and let Maya and Kaiyo know."

Maya had smiled at him as he approached her, and let him know that they were both very happy to have him join them.

The other two who made up the group of explorers were women; one had been the first to volunteer and had made her intention clear at the outset. The other had enjoyed working on building the boat and, after visiting the boat the night that Maya had addressed everyone, felt a compulsion to go.

The one who had been the first to volunteer chose to be called Talia, after a few days out at sea. She said that she felt 'tall' out on the water and as if she could touch the sky just by reaching up to it. She loved being near the sky and was a great climber, so she would often be the one climbing up the rigging to free up the sails or to keep watch.

Every day the group shared their tasks so that everyone had a chance at doing everything. Sometimes they would swap things around, if that's what they felt like doing. Kaiyo would usually be the one on first shift to steer the boat. He loved to watch the night sky greet the day sky and the stars fade as the sun threw its light above the horizon. The others, mostly, preferred to sleep at that time.

Om, as he was sometimes called by the others because he was often heard humming, never chose a name for himself. He was happy to let everyone else choose and it showed up in everything that he did. He would always allow others to choose first and was happy to be whatever he needed to be, always being on hand wherever he was needed. He also had a talent for preparing delicious meals from whatever ingredients were available.

The other woman, the one who had enjoyed building the boat, also never chose a name for herself. She loved to help everyone. She spoke rarely, yet somehow seemed to hold the group together.

Maya kept the boat shipshape. She loved to keep it clean and in good order. She would often emerge victorious from below deck after she had cleaned and tidied. Above deck, she kept the boat in good repair along with the woman who rarely spoke.

The group went about their tasks smoothly, no matter the weather, and the days went by happily, as did the nights.

Maya particularly loved the nights; the sky shone brightly on most of them. "I've never seen so many stars," she said. "I wonder what they can see? I would love to be up there with them."

Sometimes Maya felt as if she was up in the sky, shining brightly like a star, and could see everything. Her senses sharpened daily as she felt close to the elements and sensed the changes in energy of each day and night. Gradually everyone else in the group felt those changes too; the shifting colours and light in the sea and the sky, the altering feel of the wind and the boat and, eventually, the energy of everyone and everything around them. This was particularly the case when they were in shallower water. They would feel that they were close to land, and occasionally they were – only it was land that was now far beneath the water. They were to sail for close to six months before they found dry land.

One morning, there was a lot of excitement on the boat as some of the group spotted some beautiful sea creatures.

"These are dolphins," said Nala, "and I've no idea how I know that."

"They're amazing," said Kaiyo. "They can swim almost as well as you, Maya."

Maya laughed. "Almost?" she asked, and felt her laugh carry in the wind in a way that she hadn't felt before. "I feel we're nearing dry land. I can feel it in the air."

Nala agreed, as she remembered that dolphins tended to live near coasts.

The day's excitement carried through into that night and, after they ate and shared their feelings and stories, it was clear that everyone felt that they were close to dry land. No one felt like sleeping, and Maya told one of her stories from her imagination and her heart. She told a story of a gifted boy who could sing even before he was born. His mother could hear it clearly and would go around humming whatever he was singing. People could hear her humming and couldn't hear his singing, even after he was born. One day, someone thought that they could hear him and told everyone else, and then everyone else said that they could hear him too.

The group loved Maya's story and were grateful for it. They loved all her stories and slept well after them, especially that night. They were so enchanting that they helped them fall into a deep sleep and dream beautiful dreams. As everyone fell asleep, Maya saw that Nala and Om had an extra connection all of their own. Maya could see a glow of light around them and knew that their hearts were opening and flowing towards each other. It was similar to the light she had first seen coming from Kaiyo's heart even before they had come together.

As everyone's light filled the cabin that night, Maya went above deck to kiss Kaiyo before she went to sleep in her favourite spot.

He was on first watch as usual. "Maya," he said, "have you noticed how this boat is?"

"I have. It's so beautiful to feel."

"You have an amazing gift. You open up people to reach deep inside their hearts and find amazing things for themselves."

"That's not me," she replied. "That's them. I might help them along occasionally with my stories."

Kaiyo smiled. "Everyone on this boat has reached places they never thought they had. I mean, people are pretty open on Ramla,

I know that, and yet you help them to find a way of being so open, so deeply within themselves, that extraordinary things happen."

Maya was quiet for a while, reaching inside her heart. She felt that she was on an extraordinary journey into depths beyond anything that she knew.

Finally she replied. "Perhaps it's because I'm on that journey myself. And it's nice to have company."

Maya felt in her pocket for the cloth on which she had painted the makeshift map, and attempted to look at it in the dark. She could just about make out the outline. It was pure guesswork, she knew that, and she knew that they didn't need the map, even though it had seemed necessary the night they created it. She also knew that they were close to land and that it was too dark to see anything right now. She reached up and kissed Kaiyo, then walked around behind him, wrapping her arms around his back, and nuzzled her face between his shoulder blades.

She took a deep breath and felt his warmth deep down inside. "Goodnight, darling," she said.

"Goodnight, my angel," he replied and engaged the latch on the wheel. He turned around, reaching for one of the blankets he usually kept near him on his watch and wrapped it around her shoulders. He picked her up. "Goodnight, my heart," he said and kissed her.

Maya loved being picked up by him. She felt safe, warm and peaceful in his arms. She smiled and closed her eyes as he laid her down in her usual spot by the helm. She fell asleep almost instantly.

The next morning Maya was up early to take her shift, and was surprised to see Om at the wheel. "I was up early," he said, "and it's been very misty so I thought I'd relieve Kaiyo. I'd love to carry on for a little longer."

"Great," she replied. "I'll take a look around."

Maya looked over the side and could see lots of fish in the sea. "Oh, look!" she said. "Lots of fish. Lots of beautiful fish. We must follow them," and pointed in the direction that they were going.

Om was excited. "We must let the others know."

Maya was already halfway down the stairs. "I'll go and wake them." She woke Kaiyo gently, and was so excited that she could barely get the words out. "Wake up! Fish! Beautiful!" and didn't need to wake the rest of the group.

They were all excited and scrambled up on deck. As they followed the shoal of fish to shallower water for an hour, maybe a little longer, the mist began to clear and they could hear birds. Then, there it was, rising gently out of the sea, a beautiful rock right there before their very eyes. As they passed by the rock, they could see the horizon, with a beach, and people. Many people. Maya and the rest of the group waved and, for the first time in years, she had tears in her eyes.

This land was quite different to Ramla and felt much larger. Om dropped the anchor and they all got into the raft with a few of their belongings. The beach was rocky and craggy, and there were crabs and other creatures scuttling around their feet as they got off the raft. Maya was wearing a pair of sandals that one of the women on Ramla had made for her before she left; she took them off and put them in her bag. She stepped off the raft and was aware of how different she felt; she saw her feet and legs in the water and noticed how they looked and remembered the day she came to Ramla. She sensed her body again now, that of a grown woman; it was the first time she had felt it.

They were welcomed onto the land like long-lost friends. Maya looked around at the people who greeted them, lots of women and men – so many men compared to those on Ramla. There were also children, many children, and Maya was entranced by them. There had been none on Ramla.

As the group of explorers pulled the raft onto the beach, people ran into the water to help them, and the children jumped up and down in reaction to the excitement around them. The group looked at each other and smiled in acknowledgement and appreciation; they had been like a family on the boat and had shared and learnt so much. Now it was time to share with others. Maya put her hands out and held on to Kaiyo and Nala's hands, and started swinging them backwards and forwards like a little girl. Nala smiled and did the same, and soon they were all holding hands as they walked forward with big smiles on their faces. Their smiles soon turned into laughter and they were ready for their next adventure.

In the time past, before the Waters came, most people behaved differently. They didn't trust themselves and so they didn't trust others. They lacked love and respect for themselves and so for each other. They judged themselves not to be good enough, as they judged others, and many were lonely even when they were together. This brought about many internal battles and external wars and a great deal of suffering. A sense of lack was everywhere, no matter how much people had, and many people didn't seem to care that others had nothing. Most people kept themselves busy doing things so they didn't think about it. They didn't understand that keeping busy left others in charge, who liked to control, out of control.

Those in charge acted out of fear and for personal gain. They created more fear and a sense of scarcity which created a greater sense of lack. They created noise, confusion and uncertainty. This was good for a few people and they pretended it was good for everyone. They hoarded and they wasted, while thousands suffered and died without anything. They created enemies out of other fearful people, and noise to back up their stories. The noise turned into wars – so much noise and so many wars. Those who spoke of 'other ways' could barely be heard and it hardly mattered what they said because most people were too busy to listen and didn't want to care. People lost their connection with themselves and their humanity and finally … everything was washed away.

On Ramla, the Waters seemed to have brought people close to themselves and the land. Here, on the new land, it was different; people were calm and friendly, yet somehow distant. They still had a few of their possessions from before the Waters, and seemed attached to them as well as to their past. There was a sadness inside many of them, as if they were missing something from the past or looking for something in the future.

Maya would sometimes wonder about her past and whether she would ever remember it. Then she would notice the children playing and laughing and wonder why she ever wondered. The children didn't seem to wonder, and they seemed happy and free.

Maya and Kaiyo created a shelter down by the beach from abandoned material. They became as one there, in a way that transcended everything. Kaiyo had always known that Maya had an affinity with the sea, and came to realise that she was totally alive when she was near it. They spent many beautiful evenings and nights there watching the sun setting and the moon rising. They loved to watch the sky changing colour, ready for the stars to shine through. Maya loved to swim and they would often swim before going to sleep at night, to the sound of the waves.

During the day, Maya spent a great deal of time with the children. She created games, stories and a great deal of laughter. She loved the way they laughed. They often laughed until the tears rolled down their faces, which made them laugh even more. The children loved Maya's stories and pictures. She taught them to paint and write and play games and invent and make things. She learnt from them how to play and laugh until she cried.

Maya soon started noticing many changes to her body, and one of the women, who had also noticed these changes, came to speak to her. "How are you feeling?" she asked as she sat next to her on the sand.

"Happy and wonderful," replied Maya.

The woman nodded. "And how are you feeling inside?"

Maya smiled. "Happy and wonderful too."

"You love children, don't you?" the woman asked, even though she was sure of the answer.

"I do. They're so happy and I love the way they laugh and play."

"Yes, that's plain to see," said the woman, and gently placed her hand just below Maya's tummy and smiled. "And you'll soon be having one of your own. What will you call him?"

"Hassan," Maya replied without hesitation, and was surprised more at the name than the idea of having a child.

"Wonderful, we're looking forward to welcoming Hassan. I'm sure he'll be a great explorer just like his mother." The woman stood up and brushed the sand from her clothes. "You might like to consider taking up a more permanent residence before that, though. Come up and talk to us at the hall tomorrow and we'll see what we can do."

"Yes, possibly," replied Maya.

"I'll possibly see you tomorrow then," she said, and walked back up the beach.

Maya sat still for several minutes and thought about how wonderful being a child seemed to her. She felt it would be magical to be a mother and trusted that she would know how. She placed her hand just below her tummy and felt warm and hugely thankful at the thought that another human being was growing inside her.

As Maya stood up, she felt her feet and everything around her as if for the first time. She felt the wind touch her face and smiled. Inside, she was flying in a sea of beautiful colours and sounds. She turned to catch the breeze and closed her eyes and danced. She was wearing a magical gown that swirled around her. She felt it envelop her with love as she felt and saw her belly, and she loved it.

Maya opened her eyes and smiled. "Kaiyo!" she suddenly shouted. "I must let him know!" and she walked up to the houses that Kaiyo had been helping to repair.

There she was, pregnant; feeling that she'd always had an affinity with children, and yet it had never occurred to her that she might have one of her own. Now it felt like the most natural thing in the world. She felt Kaiyo close to her, touching her face and brushing her long hair aside so that he could see her as if for the first time. Although he had often done that, this time it felt like he was looking right inside her – as if he had always known. Kaiyo had been waiting for this moment and Maya didn't need to say anything.

Maya's body transformed to make way for a new life, and she marvelled at nature even though she would sometimes feel very odd inside. She liked to spend a lot of time in the water; she always felt good in the water and her body felt light. She taught the children, who were always around her, to swim and to fish, and to love the sea. She taught them how to breathe in the water and to stay down safely for as long as they wanted to. Maya would often be seen with children running around her in a circle, playing, or in the sea, swimming like a little shoal. "I want them to love the sea as I do," she would say, "and I want Hassan to love the sea as I do, too."

Kaiyo had been making a new timber-framed structure for some weeks; it was to be their new home, and a surprise for Maya. He had found many new materials on this land and had created simple building blocks from dried grasses. He knew that Maya would love them, as they had a wonderful fresh smell even after they'd been dried. Kaiyo had found a perfect spot on a hill overlooking the place where Maya loved to play with the children. Many flowers grew there and one in particular had caught his eye. It was creamy

"I want them to love the sea as I do."

yellow, a colour that he knew Maya would love, and it had soft petals and a gentle drifting scent. He was looking forward to being there with Maya and Hassan and making it their home.

It took a few weeks until, finally, with the help of many others, who were happy to do so, Kaiyo and Maya's house was ready. It was late in the afternoon and Kaiyo walked down to the beach. Maya had been playing with the children and was sitting down to rest while they were running around her, chasing each other.

"I have a new game," announced Kaiyo. The children stopped in anticipation.

Maya looked up and smiled. "Oh, what is it?" she asked, and looked around at the children, who looked slightly puzzled.

"It's a helping game," he said. "Does anyone feel like helping?" A few children nodded tentatively. "I have a surprise for Maya at the top of the hill," he continued, "and to keep it a surprise till we get there, I need a blindfold."

One girl put her hand in her pocket and pulled out a cloth that they had been using as exactly that. She shrugged her shoulders. "Easy," she said, and handed it to him.

Kaiyo smiled and took the blindfold. "Thank you," he said, and shook it vigorously to get the sand out, and the children laughed. He put it around Maya's eyes and tied it gently at the back.

"Now," he continued, "how can we get Maya up the hill safely?"

The children buzzed around Maya excitedly and she started wondering what was happening. "We'll make a chain," said one.

"What kind of a chain?" asked another.

The first one shrugged his shoulders. "A human chain," he replied, as if it was the most obvious thing in the world.

Maya got up and smiled. "What a clever idea," she said, and held out her hands in readiness.

It took Kaiyo a while to organise the children in a chain, as they all wanted to hold Maya's hand. He thought he had worked out a way in which they could all take turns to hold her hand, and then asked them to form a line going from the beach up towards the hill. He then led Maya down the line so that she was the last but one, holding two children's hands. He made his way to the top of the line and held the last child's hand. All they needed to do was have the person at the bottom of the line swap with the one at the top of the line, until they got to the top of the hill, with the exception of Maya, he explained. Whenever it was Maya's turn, the person next to her had to take her by the hand and carefully lead her to the top of the line and then take their place at the top of the line next to her. The children loved this.

When they finally made it to the top of the hill, they were all exhausted; Kaiyo and Maya too. Kaiyo took Maya's hand and led her inside. "Welcome to our new home, darling," he announced as he took the blindfold off.

"Oh!" gasped Maya as she smiled and looked around, and the children followed suit.

"It's beautiful," she said and gave Kaiyo a kiss.

"It's beautiful," the children said and started laughing.

It was a lovely spot overlooking the sea and Kaiyo and Maya were very happy there. They could also see their shelter on the beach below and would sometimes go down to it to spend the night; it was still their special spot. Somehow they came together there in a way that took them into another world. They also often bonded in their dreams and would exchange feelings, images and ideas that brought them very close to each other in their waking moments. It also brought them close to Hassan, and Maya knew that Hassan felt this.

Kaiyo treasured those nights, as he became aware of a growing restlessness in Maya and felt on occasion that she was distant. He knew that her dreams were vivid and that sometimes they stayed with her when she was awake; there was nothing unusual about that.

Now, though, she seemed to be in quite a different world, a world that he was not part of. He would always want Maya to be free, yet now he felt the possibility of losing her in a way that troubled him.

The day Maya had arrived in Ramla had transformed his life, as it had that of the whole community. She was clear and vibrant and she connected with everyone on a new level. She seemed to create 'newness' in their hearts. She brought colour into everyone's life with the emblems she painted and the clothes she made. Everyone loved how she was and how they felt after they had connected with her. She had an inner smile that was infectious, as if it had reached right inside them and left their hearts smiling too.

Kaiyo remembered the first time he had seen Maya on the beach. He'd been standing there looking out to sea. He didn't know why he was there; he just remembered that the daylight was fading. She was near a rock, close to the water's edge, and her hair was matted with sand and dried salt. She was clinging to the back of a small upturned boat and he'd put out his hand to check that she was breathing. He remembered breathing out in gratitude and relief when he felt her breath. He remembered feeling a strong bond with her. He picked her up gently and laid her on some soft grass close by so that she could be warm. He brushed her hair away from her face and wondered how long she'd been there. She must have been exhausted and yet there she was – beautiful. He remembered looking at her and feeling that he knew her; wishful thinking, maybe. He remembered looking around for something to wrap her up in, and feeling that he wanted to get her to shelter quickly.

Kaiyo also remembered how Maya had drifted in and out of sleep for weeks and how he had built her a shelter close to the beach, where he somehow knew she would want to be when she woke up. He built inside it a special plinth for her boat and made a bed out of it for her. When she finally started to respond, he remembered how he, along with Faye and Angel, had helped to get her on her feet and that she didn't seem to know how to walk. It took weeks for her to start using her feet and feel strong enough to stand up on her own. The morning after that was the first day she had walked out of her shelter, and what a day that was. Maya's graceful and childlike innocence had affected everyone from the outset.

Kaiyo then remembered how there had been no children on Ramla and, although there had been no conscious choice *not* to have them, they never came. That was just the way it was, and now there was Maya, pregnant, and soon there would be Hassan too. Kaiyo's heart filled with gratitude and his eyes with tears of joy and relief as he felt fully present to the miracle that they would soon be blessed with. He was also present to Maya and her pregnancy, and felt a new connection with her and Hassan, and breathed anew.

Kaiyo looked at Maya as she lay sleeping, her belly swollen. "Beautiful," he whispered as he knelt beside her.

Maya reached up sleepily and drew him towards her. "You too, darling," she whispered back, and they kissed.

Kaiyo lay down behind her and moulded his body to the back of hers, putting his hand gently on her belly. Maya put her hand on top of his and sighed gratefully as she felt Hassan move in response. "He's going to be a musician," she said; she often felt this when she connected with him.

"And a carpenter," added Kaiyo.

Maya smiled. "A musician and a carpenter," she said, and she felt him move again.

Maya loved to feel Hassan move, and would sometimes think of Ramla and how it would be with children. She knew that everyone there would be happy to see Hassan and felt sure that they knew about her pregnancy, especially Faye and Angel. She had learnt so much from them and would smile as she linked with each of them in her daily thoughts and activities. She connected with Faye in the plants and flowers around their new home. Maya had learnt a lot from Faye about growing plants, especially fruit trees, and had planted many in time for the next season. She connected with Angel whenever there was something to organise. She had learnt so much from her about dividing tasks and getting things done smoothly.

There were many tasks to be completed in preparation for Hassan's arrival, and both Maya and Kaiyo made beautiful things for his nursery. Kaiyo made a new baby bed and a nursing chair, and Maya made toys, bedding and cushioning. Maya would walk into the nursery and smile. "All for you, darling," she would say as she gently patted her perfectly rounded bump, and Hassan would move in response.

Kaiyo watched Maya nearing the end of her pregnancy and loved the way she was and how she looked. Although she wasn't moving around so much, she still played with the children and laughed. Her laughter was like love flowing from her veins to everyone around her. She was always beautiful and had a way of spreading beauty and joy wherever she went. It seemed to him that, the more she shared, the more she had to share. It was a joy to be around her and it was amazing to be having Hassan with her.

The night before Hassan came, Maya managed to sleep a little at a time. She would wake up to go to the bathroom, then go to the nursery to adjust something that she wanted to have just so, and get back into bed. The last time she got back into bed, she heard her waters break, and Kaiyo thought he heard it too. It was a gentle popping sound, and Maya could hardly believe it. She got up carefully and quickly and went to the bathroom.

Kaiyo got up and listened at the door. "Are you alright, darling?" he asked.

"Yes, I'm fine. Just making sure that I stay relaxed. Hassan may be a while yet."

Maya sounded calm so Kaiyo went into the kitchen to get her a drink; she liked to have some water, then fresh juice, in the morning. He sat quietly and waited for what felt to him like a very long time.

He went back to check again. "Maya—" he started to say, and before he could complete his sentence, she came out of the bathroom looking as if nothing had happened. She seemed perfectly normal. Kaiyo laughed in relief. "I was obviously expecting something," he said, "I have no idea what."

"A baby, perhaps?" Maya asked jokingly. "I'm not intending to have him all by myself."

"Always a smile," he said. "Hassan and I are very lucky."

Maya made her way into the kitchen and Kaiyo followed. She sat calmly drinking her water and juice, and all he could do was look. "Darling?" he started to ask.

"I'm not ready yet, Kaiyo. I'll let you know when I am," she said, and Kaiyo nodded and sat on a chair beside her.

Two hours later, Kaiyo felt a hand on his shoulder.

"You might want to be awake for this," said the midwife with a knowing smile. "It's a good thing Maya knew exactly when I needed to be here."

He shook his head to wake himself up. "Yes, yes," he said and stood to attention, almost falling over as he pushed the chair back.

Kaiyo put on the gown that the midwife gave him, and walked into the nursery to Maya's side. Maya had wanted Hassan to be born in his room, where she would also nurse him. She was very flushed and her long hair was stuck to her forehead and neck. Kaiyo brushed it gently aside and crouched down behind her to support her, holding both her hands as she pushed.

"Here comes the head," said the midwife. "Would you like to help?" she asked Kaiyo and Maya nodded at him quickly.

Kaiyo went over to the midwife. He could see Hassan's head in her hands. He took a deep breath and looked at her and she allowed him to take over. She instructed Kaiyo gently and Hassan seemed to know exactly what to do. As Hassan emerged into his new world, the midwife showed Kaiyo how to clear his lungs, then, suddenly, and with amazing gusto, Hassan cried the house down. Kaiyo swaddled him quickly and handed him over to Maya. An exhausted, yet elated, Maya looked at Hassan, then at Kaiyo and back again at Hassan, as she felt her energy returning to her. She had Hassan in her arms and Kaiyo at her side and felt all the blessings in this world and beyond.

"I am a very lucky lady," she said as she lay down.

The midwife smiled at Maya then looked at Kaiyo as she nodded her head. "So you are." She worked quickly to clear up so she could leave them to be together. "I'll pop by tomorrow to see how you are. Be sure to let me know if you need anything before then," she said, as she left the room and closed the door behind her.

Kaiyo lay down beside Maya while she nursed Hassan and smiled at the miracle that was Maya, Hassan and life.

Maya and Kaiyo's life was transformed by Hassan's arrival, and their love healed everything and everyone around them. They called their house Healing Waters – just as the Waters were healing the world.

Maya had learnt from Faye how a simple touch or movement of energy would get plants to respond with growth and abundant fruit. She learnt that this same transfer of energy worked its magic on people. Maya's gift – as it became known to the people around her – was a gift she gave freely. She learnt to transfer it to others so that they too could do the same. That's the way things were for Maya; she loved sharing, and Hassan was to be just the same.

People in the community took it in turns to take care of Kaiyo and Maya, bringing them food and looking after their home so that they could be free to be together and take care of Hassan. It was their time to bond and it was to be savoured.

Kaiyo knew how to take care of Hassan just as he took care of Maya. His instincts as a father, provider and protector were sublime, just like Maya's love and instincts as a mother, provider and nurturer. He had always been a great friend and lover, and now he worked his magic providing a binding energy and a loving environment for his family.

Maya would smile as Kaiyo took Hassan from her after she'd nursed him so that he could put him to sleep, or change him, or play with him. She would watch him as he stood up holding Hassan in his arms. "And there he stands, a glorious king," she would announce.

Occasionally Hassan would belch very loudly and both Maya and Kaiyo would laugh heartily. "All the man you could ever want," Kaiyo would say, and Maya felt this was exactly how she felt about Kaiyo.

Kaiyo's love for both Hassan and Maya showed in everything. He felt newly aware of his surroundings, and his skills sharpened and expanded. He had always been a talented builder and carpenter and taught many in the community to do both.

Healing Waters became a centre for the community and both adults and children came there to learn various trades. Maya taught them to create books, illustrations, paintings, fabrics and fine implements for carving and sculpting. Kaiyo made beautiful, simple furniture and, as Hassan grew, they started making musical instruments together.

Hassan loved spending time with his father in his workshop as much as he loved spending time with his mother and playing with the other children on the beach. Maya would often take them down to the bay, which she affectionately called Ramla Bay, taking a picnic with her. It had become a regular outing for the children who were not old enough to go to school, and she would sometimes be joined by one or two of the mothers. All the mothers in the community loved the way Maya interacted with their children; they seemed to learn so much from her as well as enjoy themselves.

One morning, as Maya was putting together a little picnic ready to go down to the beach with the children, she felt that something was different. She packed together a few books and pens and, as soon as the children arrived, they all went off down the hill. Everything seemed normal, with the usual laughter and games. The children ran down the hill letting the wind lift their arms, feeling as if they were about to fly. As they took the path down to the rocks to look at the creatures that clung to them, Maya noticed something quite incredible. The water had moved! It had receded a long way, and she had to look twice to see where it had gone. There was a mile of sand where the water had been, and the children didn't seem to notice. They continued on the path as normal, and she wondered if it was real or her imagination. It seemed to her to be fantastic that it could have moved so far. Could she have forgotten how far out it went at low tide? It wasn't even the right time of day for that. Perhaps they had come down a different path or to a different part of the beach? She stood still for a minute and then felt Kaiyo at her side.

"I had a feeling this morning that something was different," he said. "Perhaps we could go and explore."

"Yes, perhaps," she replied, and held Kaiyo's hand.

That night everyone gathered at Healing Waters for an evening meal. They enjoyed these gatherings and everyone would bring something to share. After they ate, Maya led the conversation. She wondered who else had noticed the water receding and when it had done so. One woman, who often went down to the beach to gather rocks and shells, said that it had happened suddenly. She had been down there the evening before and everything seemed as it had been for years.

"Actually," she said, "the bay is now almost back to what it was before the floods."

Maya felt that some people didn't want to talk about this. She asked them how they felt and they said that it didn't really matter to them where the water was; they were happy.

"I understand," she said. "I'm happy here, too." Then she asked, with a smile, "Does anyone feel like exploring?"

Three hands went up immediately. One was Kaiyo's, another was Hassan's, and the third belonged to a young girl who often came to help Maya with the children.

"Do you mean to explore by sea or land?" she asked Maya.

Maya realised that she had only considered one option. "Sea," she replied.

One of the men stood up. "I have a boat," he said, "And I would love you to use it. It's bigger than the one you came in and it's very comfortable. It survived from before the floods and is still seaworthy. I have some fuel for it, although it can sail without fuel, of course."

Maya was happy to hear this; it was the most she'd ever heard him say, "Yes, of course," she replied.

Kaiyo stood up too. "Thank you," he said. "Would you show me how to use it?"

Maya had felt for some time that her journey through life would soon take a different turn. Since Hassan's sixth birthday she had felt very strongly that there was something else for her to do, or somewhere else to be. The sudden recession of the Waters represented a major shift in energy for her, and she knew that others did not feel the same.

Maya liked to feel and see and do with her heart, and her feelings changed as her environment changed. It gave her a sense of space and wonder. Occasionally she would attempt to make sense of it in her head, and that was never where her senses were. That was Maya's world. She had never known any other. She had never known a world in which people chose to talk incessantly and never seemed to say anything; a world in which there was a lot of noise and nothing to hear; a world in which people chose to either think of their past or of their future and not be in the present. She had never known a world in which love was taken more than it was given, where many people didn't feel good enough and spent their lives attempting to fill the sense of emptiness that this created. Maya felt that the Waters had come to make a difference. She also felt that they had receded to make a difference. If others didn't feel that, it was their choice. People were free to choose.

After Maya and Kaiyo said goodbye to everyone that night, they went to put Hassan to bed. He was excited about going on an adventure, as he loved the sea. "Mummy, are we going tomorrow?"

"Not tomorrow, sweetheart. Soon. I will let you know as soon as I know. Is that okay?"

Hassan smiled and nodded as Kaiyo picked him up and hugged him. He played with his father's hair a little; he loved the way it curled. He then wriggled to indicate that he wanted to be put down; he wanted to hug his mother.

"That's okay," he said with a smile as Maya picked him up.

Hassan then played with his mother's hair so that she knew that he loved her hair too, and started humming a tune.

"Thank you, sweetheart," Maya said. "I'll stay and listen a while."

Kaiyo said goodnight and left them to it. Maya lay down next to Hassan, soothed by his humming. "It's beautiful," she said, and fell asleep next to him.

When she woke up, she walked outside to join Kaiyo. "Look at all those stars," he said. "They're amazing."

"I always want to be up there with them and see what they can see," she said. "They can see where the Waters have receded to, and what they've revealed."

"A beautiful world," he said. "So much to explore."

Maya smiled and repeated slowly, "So much to explore."

"I'll go and see that boat tomorrow; perhaps we could use it instead of the one we came in."

"Yes," she replied.

The Waters had receded in many places, revealing many new lands that had never been seen before. It had made a difference to many people, just as its coming had. They felt present to the Earth's beauty as well as to themselves and their humanity. They felt present to the beauty of life.

Maya slept soundly, as she often did before an important journey. She dreamt a magical dream that would stay in her heart for the rest of her life. She dreamt of a young girl who lived in the sea; she was a highly skilled swimmer, fast and flexible. She used her legs and feet like a beautiful tail to propel her along faster than many of the creatures in the sea.

The next morning Maya wrote down the magical tale and intended, one day, to share it with the world. She made some quick drawings and packed everything in her explorer bag, which was yellow, of course. Now she was ready whenever Kaiyo and the others were. *This is it*, thought Maya. *The journey to end all journeys.*

# CHAPTER FIVE

# Whispering Winds

Kaiyo had spent several days preparing the boat and taking it out for trips, with Hassan always at his side. Hassan was a natural sailor and knew exactly what to do. He was only six and yet seemed to anticipate every move the boat made and which way the wind would turn next.

"If he was bigger, he'd be able to handle the boat on his own," said Kaiyo. "And he loves being on the open water."

Maya was happy to hear this. "Some of the women were concerned that he may be too young."

Kaiyo smiled. "No concern needed, he's a natural. Let them come and see for themselves."

Hassan and Kaiyo had so much fun together, and everyone saw it on their faces. Others began to join them on their boat trips and very soon the group of explorers had grown to seven. They went sailing together daily, learnt easily, and enjoyed the shared energy that this created.

Maya taught them all to swim and, although some were reluctant to get in the water at first, by the time they were ready to sail they were all happy in the water. When the day came, they sailed off with little fuss and quickly got into a natural rhythm. They often saw dolphins following the boat, leaping in and out of the water, which Hassan in particular enjoyed enormously. Maya loved to see Hassan so happy around the water.

"Mum, would you teach me to jump in and out of the water like them?" he asked one day.

"Of course, sweetheart," Maya replied, realising in that moment that she could.

The rest of the group watched in amazement as Maya showed Hassan how to flex his back and legs then use his feet to propel himself out of the water. Hassan loved it. When she taught him how to dive back in again smoothly, the rest of the group was keen to learn. Maya was so at home in the water, her ease helped the others to feel the same and learn quickly. She taught them one by one, then in a group, and soon they were all jumping in and out of the water as if they had been born to it. It was a magical time and the group would often get in the water and swim with the dolphins.

Kaiyo was also very at home with and in the water. Maya had observed this at Healing Waters, as well as on Ramla, once they had chosen to go exploring. He was a natural sailor and would take charge of the boat while the others went swimming at the end of the day. He had taught everyone to sail beautifully, and they had all become proficient sailors. He was the quiet core of the group and felt energised by the way everyone interacted.

Apart from Maya, Kaiyo and Hassan, there were two young women and two men, one of whom was the boat owner's son. Maya and Kaiyo had also taught them to fish, which supplemented their provisions nicely. They all loved being on the boat and were very happy, perhaps even reluctant to get back to land.

"People are funny," Maya would say to Kaiyo. "First they're reluctant to take to the water, then they're reluctant to get back to land." For Maya there was never an issue; the land and the water were both an integral part of her and she was happy on either.

Hassan was happy wherever he was, and flourished on this journey. He loved to feel the wind against his face and in his hair and the water against his skin. He loved its saltiness and the little

They sailed off with little fuss

white marks it sometimes left. He grew taller, and ate and slept well. He was an active member of the group and loved taking care of the boat. He also loved to create music with the two instruments he had brought with him. One was small and flute-like, only wider than a flute, and was made of a light wood. It made light, yet deep, hollow sounds depending on how he held it or blew into it. The other was a wooden block that was the first instrument he had made; his father had helped him shape it from a piece of wood that he liked. He would simply tap it with sticks that he made from different materials to create different sounds. It had always been his favourite, and he would sometimes ask his mother to play it for him while he was falling asleep.

One morning Maya asked Hassan about his dreams. "Do you dream while you're sleeping, sweetheart?"

"Sometimes," he replied. "And at other times I dream when I'm awake."

"Oh? What kind of dreams?"

Hassan told Maya about a dream he'd been having a lot lately. He had first dreamt it the night before they had sailed away from Healing Waters. He told her how, in his dream, he lived with the fish and other creatures in the water and how he'd made friends with them all and swam and ate just like they did. Maya was fascinated by the detail with which he described all the creatures, and asked him if he would like to draw them. That afternoon they spent time drawing some of the creatures and Maya sketched one out as Hassan described it. It was a whale, and Maya was intrigued. As Hassan coloured it in, he left a distinctive white mark on its forehead.

Maya picked it up. "Who's this, sweetheart?"

"It's Kiriyu, Mum," he replied matter-of-factly.

"Kiriyu. You know that name?"

"Yes, I know him from your dreams."

"Oh, I've told you about him?"

"Well, not exactly, I just see him in your dreams."

"You see him from my dreams? How do you mean?" She knew that she and Kaiyo had shared dreams when they slept in the beach hut, yet it had never occurred to her, in all the time she had spent falling asleep with Hassan, that they might have done the same.

"It happens when we fall asleep together, or when we dream when we're awake."

Maya smiled at Hassan and shook her head. "Wow, how lucky am I?"

"Me too, Mum. I like your dreams," he replied as he playfully put his arm around her shoulder and kissed her cheek.

"Tell me about my dream with Kiriyu."

"It's the same as my dream. You're living in the water with him and the other whales and sea creatures. That's how you know to swim so well."

"Let's go for a swim before bedtime," she suggested, "and join the sea creatures."

Maya and Hassan spent more time together in the water after that conversation. The more time Maya spent in the water, the more she became aware of Kiriyu and her dream and, that she had dreamt this dream many times. Kaiyo would occasionally join them for a swim and it was amazing to see them melt together in joy, laughter and love. Their bond was strong and constantly growing and it would never break.

The group of explorers had spent several weeks out at sea now, and the dolphins were long gone. The boat owner's son was taking the helm more often and, as Maya sensed that they were getting close to land, she also observed a difference in everyone else's behaviour. The whole group sensed it, although subconsciously.

Maya spoke to the group one night to let them know. "I feel we're very close to land," she said. They all smiled and were silent for several minutes until the boat owner's son finally said, "We'd like to stay on the boat," and looked over at one of the young women, the one who used to come and play with the children and help Maya at Healing Waters. He smiled.

The woman looked at Maya. "We'd like to go ashore with you; we'll get some provisions then sail on for a while longer."

"We could come back for you," said the boat owner's son.

"That would be great," said Maya. "Although we may be here for a while, we might like to go back to Healing Waters." Maya nodded and looked at both Kaiyo and Hassan, who both responded with a slight shrug of their shoulders.

"Come back when you're ready," she said and smiled.

Two days later, in the early evening, they could see land; a very different land. There were boats and people and many houses, as well as lights. They looked at each other with questioning eyes and for a moment they all wanted the same thing – to turn around and go back. At the same time, they wanted to go ashore and explore, just as they had intended. Hassan went to each person on the boat and hugged them and, as he did so, they smiled and felt bound together more than ever. They knew that they would be there for each other, even when they were apart.

Hassan had an amazing gift for bonding people; his love for them was open, boundless and trusting. It helped them to trust themselves, and just as Maya did with people on Ramla, he passed to them his innocence and joy.

As the group drew nearer to the shore, Kaiyo put down the anchor and lowered the dinghy for everyone to get into. They rowed it to shore and no one on the beach seemed to notice their arrival. *Perhaps they have people coming ashore all the time*, thought Kaiyo.

They pulled the dinghy ashore and Kaiyo secured it to a large rock with a rope. He looked up and for a moment was unsure what to do next. This place was very different from anything he had experienced before. He looked at Maya and Hassan and smiled, put his bag over his shoulder and held their hands as the group walked up to the nearest building.

"Good evening," Kaiyo said to the man behind the shop counter. "We've travelled a long way, and wondered where we might get food and shelter for the night?"

"Oh, did you now?" he said. "We sell beach stuff here and the odd snack." He pointed to a few items in a basket. "If you're after somewhere to stay, there's a B&B two miles down the road. I know the owner, Jim, and I'm sure he'd have room for you all – that's if you're all together?" he asked, looking around at the group.

"Oh, yes, we're together," replied Kaiyo. "And thank you."

"Don't mention it," said the man, who had already turned away to do something else.

None of the group knew what a 'B&B' was – as long as it provided them with food and shelter, though, they were happy. While walking down the road, they saw many things that they did not recognise. There were cars, motorbikes and bicycles, among many other things. People seemed very busy and no one looked at them. Eventually they came to a sign at the side of the road: *Harbour – your friendly B&B*. As they walked through the entrance into a reception area they saw a man behind a desk and heard strange chaotic music playing in the background.

"Hello, are you Jim?" asked Kaiyo.

"Depends who's asking," said Jim, and laughed very loudly.

Kaiyo wasn't quite sure how to reply to that question. "I am," he said eventually.

Jim laughed even louder than before. "Okay, so what can I do for you?"

"Well, we're simply after food and shelter for the night."

"Where are you from?" asked Jim, who seemed to talk in questions.

"We've travelled from another land," said Maya. "And we thought we might stay a while and explore, perhaps set up home here for a while and get to know everyone."

"Everyone?" said Jim, suppressing another laugh. "That might take a long while." No one else laughed, so he sighed then continued. "Well, I'm guessing you'll want three rooms. I have a nice big one for you, your husband and little boy," said Jim, looking at Maya. "I'll charge you all the same rate though."

"Charge?" asked Maya. "I'm not sure what you mean?"

"Well, I would normally charge ninety for each room and one hundred and twenty for the larger one. With things being quiet, though, you can have them for sixty each, so that'll be one hundred and eighty altogether."

The whole group looked puzzled. They weren't sure what he was talking about, and turned to walk out. "Wait," said a voice in the background. "Jim, just let them stay."

Jim shook his head. "Woman, you'll be the ruin of me and this business yet!" he said, then handed over three sets of keys.

The person to whom the voice belonged, who was going to be the 'ruin of Jim and this business yet' came out from behind a door and round the counter to show them to their rooms.

"Things have been a bit strange," she said as she walked up the stairs. "This was a thriving little business once, and we thought the water had taken it all away. Jim was so happy when the water settled back, and he's spent a long time restoring as much of it as he could. It's not a patch on what it used to be; it's our home, though, and business, of course, and you're welcome to stay."

Maya smiled in appreciation. "Thank you," she said as the woman opened a room for Maya, Kaiyo and Hassan and handed Maya the key.

"I'll see you in the morning," the woman said. "If you need anything before then just come down to the desk."

After she showed the others to their rooms, she went back downstairs and gave a slightly puzzled looking Jim a kiss. "Thank you." she said, and he sighed.

They all slept that night, although not as well as usual. As well as the lurching feeling they had when they lay down, as a result of being at sea for so long, there was this strange place with its strange people. This was going to be some adventure.

The next morning the woman who had shown them to their rooms made them breakfast. Her name was Mary and she was Jim's wife. They were all very grateful to her and wondered what they could do to repay her kindness, since it seemed that people didn't get food and shelter here in the way that they were used to.

They found out that people used a thing called 'money' to buy things, and that they first had to do something to get money, so that they could buy things with it. It seemed complicated to them, as did a great many other things that filled people's lives here. It seemed to them that while people had a lot of things, some very useful, such as fuel for engines, they had little time for themselves or for each other.

The boat owner's son, who called himself Mark, stayed on long enough to get some fuel for the boat and some provisions, and sailed off with the young woman who had become known as Jess. The other two explorers joined a farmer who was interested in learning from them what he called 'traditional farming methods', and they were happy to help.

Maya, Kaiyo and Hassan stayed on with Jim and Mary until they made a home of their own. There were many abandoned buildings that needed work and Maya, Kaiyo and Hassan chose two close to the beach. Many other buildings were in a better state of repair, although they were not so close to the beach.

Mary and Maya spent a lot of time together, walking on the beach and exchanging stories. Maya learnt many things from Mary, including how the floods – or the Waters, as she still sometimes called them – had happened, as well as how and why they had started to recede. She learnt how people lived and worked and how they were paid with money so that they could buy things, including their homes. She also learnt that there wasn't much work or money around, because of how the floods had affected what Mary called the 'world economy'. Maya didn't understand why it had to be that way, and both women were fascinated with what the other had to say about this; and soon they became very good friends.

Maya, Kaiyo and Hassan loved being close to the beach and Maya's love flowed in abundance and showed in everything she did. Her creativity also flowed and she wrote, painted and invented, and made many wonderful things. She created a new set of paints from natural materials she had found. She had a whole new palette of colours to reflect this new land and its riches. Her paintings had a healing quality which, to most people, seemed to come from beyond their world; to Maya, it came from deep within it.

Hassan created music and, with his father's help, made new instruments. His creativity showed in his designs and in the sounds that he produced from them. Kaiyo became a boat-builder and people came from far and wide to see his unusual boats and commission new ones. He designed and built them from his heart. People loved the way they looked and handled. They were beautifully balanced and they were fast, at one with the wind and the water. Both whispered past them and guided them through their journey. The boatyard and the house became known as Whispering Winds.

This new land was full of new experiences for the group and new ways of being. People watched television and seemed to relate to it in a sleep-like way; they said it wasn't as good as it used to be.

They had cars to take them to near and faraway places, although most chose to stay close to their homes. The ones who had what they called 'work' seemed to work hard to be rewarded with money so that they could get things that seemed important to them. They said that the floods had changed them and that their things were less important than before. They said that family was important, and yet seemed always busy and disconnected from themselves and their families.

Maya had a sense of how things might have been had she lived there before the Waters came. She got to know about relationships with mothers, fathers, sisters and brothers. She got to know about daughters and sons and wives and husbands, and wondered what kind of daughter she might have been. She started to have a strong sense of her mother and father. She knew that she was teaching Hassan her ways, and so was Kaiyo, and felt that how she was – even after the Waters came – must have had something to do with the way her parents had been. She loved that feeling. She felt that they were with her, and smiled as she felt the warmth in her heart. She smiled as she thought of Faye and Angel and Ramla. She smiled as she thought of Healing Waters. She smiled as she thought of the sea and its creatures and the sun and the moon and the stars. She smiled as she thought of the wind. She smiled as she thought of Kaiyo and Hassan, and now Whispering Winds. She smiled as she thought of this land and its people. She smiled as she thought of Mary and the way she had taken them in.

Mary seemed different to the others they had met on this land; she had a light energy and was open and sharing. It showed in her body and in the way she connected with people, and it showed in the way she laughed. Mary and Maya loved to laugh together and, the more time they spent together, the younger Mary looked and felt.

Today, Maya and Mary were off early for a picnic and Mary had lent Maya a bicycle, or bike, as she often called it. They had been cycling a few times together and even though Maya didn't have a bike, she had learnt to ride quickly. She would also cycle up hills as if they weren't there. This never seemed to deter Mary, who often got off her bike to walk up the last bit of a hill. This morning, they took their supplies and waved goodbye to Kaiyo and Hassan who were preparing to go sailing with friends. As they rode off, Mary suggested to Maya that they opened a school together.

"What kind of school?" asked Maya, who had chosen to teach Hassan at home after a few days at the local school.

"A different kind of school," replied Mary.

"Here, they put children in small rooms and expect them to sit still all day and listen and write things and then remember them," Maya said.

"I know," said Mary. "It's been like that for as long as I can remember, and we didn't take the opportunity to change things after the floods. For a while it looked as if no one was going to attend school; the children didn't want to go – hardly a surprise – and many of the parents weren't pushing them either. Anyhow, after a lot of pushing and shoving, they got the children back to school – only just though. They stopped the preschool classes and, as they called it, 'focused' on the older children."

Mary paused, waiting for a reaction from Maya, who just nodded. "We could teach them the way you teach Hassan and the way you teach me. Many of the mothers have been asking me about you and wanted to know if you would teach their children."

"That's strange," said Maya. "No one's ever mentioned it."

"They're a little scared of you."

Maya started laughing. "I know," she said, attempting to pull a scary face, "I am a scary woman!"

Mary was laughing too. "It's no joke," she said, attempting to compose herself. "They wonder how you stay in such good shape and look so young without making an effort. That's a little scary for most women – men too, come to think of it – although most of them would do almost anything to be with you."

"Be with me?" asked Maya. "Most of them don't like being with themselves, so how can they expect to *be* with anyone else?"

Mary nodded, "Exactly!" she agreed, and then continued. "I had the idea of also doing adult evening classes to teach people how to be together. I get your point though, we should teach them how to be with themselves first."

Maya looked at Mary and started to laugh again. "Listen," she said. "I'd like to stay on my bike, so will you please stop making me laugh?"

"I will not," said Mary. "Why should I? Besides, it's good exercise – the laughing, I mean."

Maya and Mary laughed so much that they laughed their way to the top of the hill. This was quite an achievement for Mary, who had never managed to cycle up it before without getting off her bike and pushing at least some of the way.

"Wow!" Mary said. "How did you do that?"

"I didn't – you did!"

The women got off their bikes and laid them on the grass.

"You see," Mary said as she took a blanket out of her bag for them to sit on, "that's exactly what I mean. That's why you need to teach people."

"I'm not sure how," said Maya, as she helped Mary with the blanket and sat down. "It's natural to me. How can you teach people to be natural if it doesn't come naturally to them?"

"Hmmm," Mary was thinking. "I see what you mean." She sat down beside Maya, and continued. "I'm sure we can figure something out, and it would make a big difference to this community."

Maya loved Mary's idea and thought since it was such a good one, something would come to her to make it happen.

"So, who first? The adults or the children? And do the adults want to do this? People don't learn things well unless they want to."

"We could call it *Forever Young*," said Mary. "That will get them flocking, although they may be expecting some lotions and potions rather than anything that they need to do."

"That's the odd thing, you see. They don't need to do anything. That's what they need to learn – to let things happen naturally. It's almost as if they need to *unlearn*. It seems strange, I know," said Maya. "It took me a while to know this."

"That's great," replied Mary. "I love it. It might take a while to know how to 'unteach' them though."

Maya sat up. "I have an idea."

Three days later, Mary and Maya put posters up all over town and dropped leaflets through every door with the help of a few friends.

**FOREVER YOUNG**
*Learn how to be energised and vital,
get fit, and look and feel young with little effort.
Tonight and every Tuesday night at
Whispering Winds between 7 and 10 P.M.
Also enjoy some of Mary's home-baked
cakes along with Maya's special tea.*

By 6.45 that evening, Maya and Mary couldn't believe their eyes. At least a couple of hundred people had turned up.

"I think we hit the spot," said Mary.

"You might have to bake more cakes," said Maya.

"No way," replied Mary. "I'm not missing a single minute of this!"

The evening was a riot. After enjoying Maya's special tea and Mary's cakes in the meeting room, everyone went through to the large craft room. Maya had laid objects all over the floor and showed them what they needed to do. They needed to be like babies, she explained – seeing, exploring and discovering simple things for the first time. They weren't allowed to speak and had to crawl around picking one object at a time. They had three minutes to play with each object and when Maya blew a whistle they had to move on to the next one, or wait their turn for another, as there weren't enough to go round. The objects were of many different shapes, sizes, colours and textures, and some made noises, much to everyone's amusement.

Mary was amazed that everyone joined in so willingly. "What did you put in that tea of yours?" she asked after everyone had gone.

"Wouldn't you like to know!" replied Maya.

"You should sell it."

Maya laughed. "I will, as long as I can grow it and get Kaiyo and Hassan to dry it fast enough."

"You're kidding me, aren't you?" Mary knew the answer to that question before she'd even asked it; she knew that Maya had green fingers and could grow just about anything,

"Now, there's another idea."

Maya put her hands up as if to stop Mary. "Slow down!" she said.

Mary laughed. "Well, I never thought I'd hear that from Superwoman!"

Everyone had had a great night. They enjoyed themselves so much and Mary said she had never seen them quite like that before. She loved seeing the community open up in that way. Many people stayed to help clean up afterwards and said they were looking forward to the next one.

Mary and Maya's classes grew in popularity and, just as Maya had intended, once the adults felt what it was like to be naturally themselves, it was easy to pass this on to others.

Many of the parents were keen to have Maya teach their children, and eventually she started a preschool class. It wasn't all plain sailing; she had a lot of opposition from the 'powers that be', as Mary called them. They let Maya know that her application was unusual and that she would normally need qualifications to run a preschool. They then conceded that because of the 'hiccup' in the teacher-training system, which meant she wouldn't be able to get any qualifications, they would give her application careful consideration.

"She doesn't teach them anything," said one woman. "They just play about all day and laugh a lot, as if that's going to work."

One of the men agreed. "Her methods might be okay for the preschool stage. She must not be allowed to open a junior school though. Her methods would not be appropriate for that, in my humble opinion."

"She hasn't applied for a junior school," replied another man.

"She might if we let her open a preschool," said the first woman.

"Maya is a very capable woman," said another woman. "I wasn't sure about her at first, and now I know that if she says she can do something, then she can. I feel we should allow her to give it a go. Lord knows we're barely holding on at the moment."

"That's no reason to let people do whatever they want," said the first woman. "She always seems a little odd to me. No one's meant to be that happy all the time. It's not natural, and neither is that tea of hers."

"Well, we could just insist that the children aren't given it. Just in case," proposed the second woman.

Two days later Maya's tea plants and all her tea were confiscated and taken to a laboratory to check for illegal content. Nothing of the sort was found, and things went very quiet for a while. Many of the parents who knew Maya were still determined to have her teach their children, so they pursued her school application and lobbied until eventually the board relented and let them have their school.

The preschool was allowed to open under strict supervision. The board members supervised the classes closely and sat in on them to satisfy themselves that nothing untoward was happening. Many believed that the classes would do little to educate the children, and that at least they were being kept out of trouble until something more traditional could be fully implemented. Other board members were very impressed by the way Maya connected with and engaged the children. They had fun and learnt things like practical mathematics, plant biology and how to use natural materials to create useful objects.

The town became a vibrant and prosperous place and people came from far and wide to buy produce, including Maya's tea, attend classes and see Whispering Winds. Many communities were also interested in understanding how this worked, and how they could do the same in their own communities. Education boards were interested in how Maya's classes worked for both children and adults, and wanted to repeat them elsewhere.

Jim, who had initially opposed anything to do with Kaiyo or Maya, eventually warmed to them. Mary had no doubt benefited from being with Maya, and Jim could not fail to see the differences it had made in her. At one point, he had become concerned that if he didn't join in she might leave him for a younger man.

Mary and Jim completed all the renovations to their premises, adding a big hall to house the large classes they held there and several more rooms to accommodate the people who attended them. Jim became the proud owner of a very successful hotel and Mary a thriving homemade cake business. Maya and Kaiyo had transformed the lives of the community and everyone whom they knew in less than a year. It was to be another year before they would have any thoughts of moving on. It was a significant year for many reasons, and it also marked the first time that Maya and Kaiyo had a major disagreement.

Maya loved being part of creating the transformation that was Whispering Winds and, along with Mary, ran classes to pass on her teaching methods. She knew that other communities were struggling to create a life that they loved and she was keen to go and help them.

Kaiyo did not agree. "Not everyone wants to be transformed, Maya, and we're happy here."

"Surely you would want to help other communities?" she asked.

"We are helping them, Maya, with what we have here. I love what I'm doing and I thought you did too. And Hassan is happy here."

"Hassan is happy wherever we are, Kaiyo."

Kaiyo detected a change in Maya's energy and looked at her. "I know, Maya, and I thought we were happy here."

"We are, Kaiyo, it's just—"

She took a breath and didn't know how to explain why she felt she needed to be somewhere else. This was a strange feeling for Maya; she'd been so used to Kaiyo knowing how she felt and, feeling the same way. *So now what?* she asked herself. *I feel I need to be somewhere else and he feels he needs to stay here.* She wondered if perhaps it was time for them to make a different choice, at least for a while.

Over the next few days Maya spent a lot of time in and on the sea. She often took one of the smaller boats out by herself and would anchor somewhere along the coast to be with her feelings and to swim; she loved to swim. The classes and the school now had plenty of helpers and she would occasionally be there to guide them. Hassan was occupied during the day at Maya's new school, along with his friends. Kaiyo was busy with his boats and clients. She was yearning to invent and create new things, and she felt she needed to be somewhere new to do that, although she wasn't sure where.

Maya understood what Kaiyo had said, and he had made clear his choice, and that was to stay; and Maya chose to do the same until her choice was clear to her. Maya knew that Kaiyo loved her and she loved him. She knew that he'd always been there for her and that she'd never before had to ask him to do anything; he always seemed to know what to do and when to do it. She wanted to be with him and Hassan and to explore new places and she now accepted that this might not be possible. She started to write and paint again, usually down in the bottom shed, closest to the beach. She kept some paints and brushes there, along with an easel that Kaiyo had made for her, so she that could paint and be close to the sea whenever she wanted to.

One morning, as she sat outside the shed on the beach playing with the sand, she noticed the water pooling around her toes and had a clear image of the day that she had arrived on Ramla. She remembered looking at the water and the sand swirling around her feet; it had felt like a dream. Then she remembered her dream about the young girl who had lived in the water with the sea creatures. She'd always felt she was that girl and now, for the first time ever, it felt like something other than a dream – it felt real. She remembered the water and learning to dive and how the water felt on her skin. She remembered coming up for air and how it felt in her nostrils. She remembered many things and, as the images came, she started to paint. As she painted one image, another would come, and another, and another, waiting to be painted. She couldn't stop painting, and felt herself melt into her images. She felt sleepy and didn't notice the tears streaming down her face until she closed her eyes. She felt herself falling towards the ground and never reaching it. She felt suspended somewhere between her dreams and reality.

Maya woke up the next morning wondering if her day on the beach, with all the images and the paintings and the tears, had been a dream. She got out of bed feeling odd, and took her time showering. Kaiyo had left Maya a note:

*Walking Hassan round to the big classroom. Back shortly.*
*Wait for me to have breakfast. I LOVE YOU*

Maya sat on the bed motionless for several minutes; she thought she had lost Kaiyo. She thought she would have to leave without him and that they no longer wanted the same things. She also thought about Hassan and how he loved the sea, and loved exploring, just like her. She loved them both dearly and could not imagine her life without them. At that moment Kaiyo walked into the room.

"Maya," he said, "I thought I had lost you."

"What do you mean?"

"You left without a word; you were gone for days."

"Gone? Gone where? I was down by the beach in the bottom shed painting."

"Maya, you took one of the boats out, I thought you and Hassan had gone and he was only with Mary as usual and—"

Maya interrupted. "Well, of course he was with Mary. I walked him down to his class."

"You were nowhere to be found," Kaiyo continued.

"I was in the bottom shed painting," she said.

"Maya, you weren't there! We couldn't find you anywhere. You took one of the boats out and you were gone for days!"

Maya didn't understand what she was hearing. That wasn't what she thought had happened!

"And the paintings?" she asked. "Did you see the paintings?"

Kaiyo softened his voice, "There were no paintings, Maya." He put his arms around her. "You haven't touched your paints for days."

Maya knew that Kaiyo always said things the way they were. She trusted him implicitly. "Okay," she said, sinking back into the bed. "There were no paintings." Suddenly she sat up, "I'd better start painting, then." And they both laughed.

Kaiyo was relieved. "Not before you've had some breakfast," he said. "You haven't eaten for days."

"That's what you think; I had all the food I ever needed."

Kaiyo and Maya ate breakfast and walked down to the bottom shed. They spent the day together, Maya painting and Kaiyo carving a piece of wood he was preparing for one of the boats.

"What are you carving?" she asked.

"Oh, something to go on the boat. I found this old compass and thought it would be fun to use it to navigate. It'll be finished by the end of the day and I can test it out tomorrow and teach Hassan how to use it. He can't wait."

"Okay," she said in a slightly preoccupied way. "Hassan loves the sea."

"He's just like you," Kaiyo said smiling. "A total natural, as if he'd spent his life in it."

"Darling," said Maya, "come and look at this painting."

Kaiyo looked over at the painting. It was of a young girl with long wavy brown hair and a flowing pale yellow gown. It swirled around her body and legs and she seemed to be dancing in the water with what looked like a whale.

"Do you know who this is?" she asked.

"It's you, darling."

"I meant the whale," she said, smiling.

Kaiyo smiled too. "Yes, it's Kiriyu."

"We spent a lot of time together when I was out at sea," Maya said. "Sit down, please, I'd like to share some things with you."

Kaiyo sat on the floor and Maya squeezed in beside him and started to recount her story clearly. She remembered her father and what he looked like. She remembered the day he died and how sad her mother was for two years afterwards. She remembered the house they had lived in, her school, her friends and her fifth birthday party. She remembered how she came to know about the 'walking' whales. She remembered the story she had written about Kiriyu and his tribe, and Malika, his mother. She told him about the sheer delight she had felt when her mother announced their journey to the desert to see the valley where all the whale skeletons had been found. She told him how she had packed her little yellow rucksack that her father had given her. She told him about her love–hate relationship with the colour yellow.

"Wow!" he said. "I always knew that there was a story behind that colour."

She told him about the skeletons of all the sea creatures and the one she thought belonged to Kiriyu. She told him how she had wished that they would all be alive again in the sea and not dead and dried up. She told him how she had wished so hard that she had made the Waters come, and that she felt responsible for all that had happened.

"Maya," he said softly, "you're not responsible for the Waters."

"When I was a young girl," she said, "I would dream so much, even when I was awake, and sometimes I couldn't tell my imagination from reality. Then, my father died, and in my dreams and my imagination he was still alive, and we read, and we wrote, and we drew, and we laughed, and we painted – just like before. He would be there when I came home from school, and especially on special days like birthdays. I sometimes felt that other people could see him too, especially Mum, although she never said so. In my dreams he was alive and I wanted my dreams and my reality to be the same. You see, I never got to say goodbye to him, and he never went anywhere without saying goodbye."

Maya leant her back against the wall. She was exhausted. Kaiyo sat motionless for a few seconds, watching the tears roll down her cheeks. Then he took the brushes and the paints gently out of her hands and placed them on the easel. He put his arms around her and held her close. He could feel her breath against his chest and her hair brush past his cheek as she buried herself in his embrace. It had been some time since they had been so close, and they melted together as if for the first time, as if nothing could ever separate them. Love did not describe it; it did not even come close.

Kaiyo knew how to please Maya in so many ways; she was an integral part of him and he felt alive when he was with her. He felt like the king of the world. He had made a choice on Ramla to be with her always and he knew what that meant. He had always found it easy to feel what was in people's hearts; it was one of his gifts after the Waters came. He felt Maya's heart as clearly as if it were his own, and that was a gift all on its own. He knew about her 'journeys' even when she didn't. She wasn't always consciously aware of them. They were usually short, a day or two at most, and she shared them with him in many ways. They were magical journeys and she usually emerged victorious, renewed and full of creativity and vitality.

Maya's journeys were part of her beauty, a beauty that transcended everything Kaiyo had ever known. He knew that Maya did not always distinguish between reality and her imagination, and felt that she would come to remember something from her past when she was ready. This last journey had been different. It had lasted six days and Kaiyo feared she might be gone forever. There was something different about each journey, only this time Maya was different. She was aware that her story was from something other than her imagination. She knew it was from her past, from before the Waters.

As Maya shared her remarkable story with Kaiyo, she felt for the first time that it was *her* story. She talked about the day she came to Ramla and how she had not been sure whether she was dead or alive. She talked about how she came to be there and how Kiriyu had helped her. She talked about how Kiriyu had always been in her dreams or her imagination, even before Hassan had brought him to her consciousness and how she now felt him to be real. She talked about how often her dreams or imagination and reality got mixed up, and that she was just starting to 'unmix' them. As Kaiyo listened to Maya and felt her heart, he knew that her next journey would be her biggest. He knew that it would be a journey deep into her heart and that he and Hassan would be with her.

Kaiyo had often felt like an observer in Maya's world, a world so different to anyone else's who had survived the Waters. The Waters had created an extraordinary world and extraordinary people, and yet Maya still stood out. He knew that he was not the only one to feel this; Angel and Faye had felt it immediately and eventually so had everyone else who knew her. Kaiyo felt ready. He had already started to prepare the boat for what was to be their final journey on the Waters, and their first passage deep into Maya's world.

Kaiyo asked Maya if she would take him swimming and help him to be at one with the sea again. The sea always felt different to him when he was with Maya. It felt as if it was in his body; it felt a part of him. After a few daily swims together, he felt his senses amplified by the water. On land, he also felt his senses enlivened; the ground felt at one with his feet, as if it walked *with* him. His body felt young, strong, flexible and vibrant. He was ready for the journey.

# CHAPTER SIX

# Maya's Journey

It was quite a gathering, and it would be Maya, Kaiyo and Hassan's last at Whispering Winds. Their gatherings were popular and many people came, bringing food and drink. Mary felt that there was something different about this gathering and, as soon as she arrived, she made her way straight to the kitchen to talk to Maya.

"What's this about?" asked Mary.

"I think Kaiyo has something in mind," Maya replied.

"Really?" she said. "And what do you have in mind?"

"It's a strange thing. A few days ago I had a dream that woke me up."

Mary was concerned. "You mean a nightmare?"

"Well, not quite. I mean, it helped me see and feel things in a different way. I felt that I had woken up from a long dream and that I needed to be back with the sea to go on a journey, or perhaps complete one that I've been on all my life."

"You mean the little trip with the boat when you disappeared for days?"

"Actually, I wasn't aware that I had gone anywhere," replied Maya. "I thought it was a dream. The funny thing is, I've felt for a while that I needed to go on this journey."

"You felt *you* needed to go on this journey? Were you planning to go on your own?"

"Yes," said Maya, "that was a possibility."

"What kind of journey?" Mary asked. "Are you leaving us?"

"I think we might. I've left it up to Kaiyo to choose. He always knows when the time is right."

"You will wait a while, won't you? You will let it settle?" Mary was upset at the thought of Maya leaving. "I'm sorry, I'm asking you a lot of questions. I should mind my own business. I really don't want you to go and I was wondering what was behind it and if it was something I could help with."

Maya smiled. "Thank you, Mary. You're a wonderful friend."

"Then stay," she replied.

"Mary, this dream has somehow brought back memories from before the Waters. They're still fragmented and I feel a need to be on the water to put them back together."

"Back together? That doesn't sound like you," Mary was puzzled. "And does Kaiyo feel the same?"

"He didn't at first. I mean, before I went off on my little trip, as you call it, and now I feel that he might."

Mary had tears in her eyes. She had always known that Maya and Kaiyo wouldn't stay forever and was surprised that they had stayed so long. She had hoped that, since Hassan had settled so well there, they would choose to stay longer. Despite her upset, she was also happy that they were choosing to do this together, whatever 'this' might be. She smiled at Maya then helped her take some food into the large meeting room.

Kaiyo was sitting in the corner talking to Jim, and Mary wondered what they might be talking about. *They'll have a lot to organise before they go*, she thought, *and who would look after the boatyard? No one else has Kaiyo's skills.* She thought about how Kaiyo had passed on his skills and, although most people did not have his instincts, they had learnt well. *It's not the same as having an instinct for something, though*, she thought as she smiled and nodded at both Jim and Kaiyo and passed them some food trays. *Instinct,* she thought, *that's what Kaiyo and Maya have brought to Whispering Winds – an instinct for so many things. Between them they have managed to bring out people's natural talents or somehow transfer theirs to them. Either way, this community has been transformed by their presence.*

Mary remembered many things that Maya had said as she walked to and from the kitchen carrying food. She remembered how Maya felt that what some saw as her extraordinary talents were natural instincts. She said she felt that everyone had them and that sometimes they were covered up. She said that people could choose at any time to let them be uncovered. She said that sometimes, when they had been covered up for a long time, it was brave to let them be uncovered. She said that the way for that to be easy was to keep our hearts open. She said that our open hearts were the gateway to a boundless source of life, energy and countless other natural instincts.

Mary also remembered what Maya had said about people needing to trust themselves and be at ease with their natural instincts so that they could trust others and give them the space to do the same. Maya, Kaiyo and Hassan had helped people to feel and be at ease with themselves and others – that was the transformation – and Mary had never felt it so clearly before. *That's why everyone feels so good around here!* she thought.

"Why?" asked Maya.

Mary was surprised. "Why what?"

"You said 'That's why everyone feels so good around here.'"

Mary laughed. "I didn't realise I'd said it out loud."

"You didn't," said Maya. "I still heard you, though."

"That's why I love you so much, Maya. You seem to know me without me having to say a thing. I know, that's how we all are naturally, right? It's funny how being natural got so difficult."

"That's the thing, though, Mary, it isn't. It's easy. If we can just get over it and be with it."

The two women smiled as they walked back into the meeting room with the last of the food trays. They sat on a bench and squeezed up next to each other. Mary put her arm around Maya.

"Listen up, everyone," said Kaiyo as he stood up and turned to face everyone with Jim still at his side. "I have some great news." Everyone turned around to listen.

"Ooh, here we go," said Mary.

Kaiyo continued. "Maya, Hassan and I are going to go off exploring, and we'd love you to take care of Whispering Winds for us. Jim has agreed to take care of the boatyard and he was wondering if anyone else would like to help. You'd be running it as if it were your own business."

A few hands went up. "Please speak to Jim," said Kaiyo, and Jim nodded.

"How long are you planning to be away for?" asked one of the young men who put up his hand.

"Indefinitely," Kaiyo said with a flourish. "We're not planning on coming back. Maya and Hassan are great adventurers and I am at their service."

The room was quiet for a few seconds and then Jim stepped forwards. "Wow," whispered Mary to Maya. "That's Jim. The man I love."

"The day Kaiyo and Maya came ashore," Jim said, "I wanted them to leave. They couldn't pay their bill for a start!" He smiled as he remembered and others chuckled as they remembered the old Jim who used to complain about everything.

"Within days," he continued, "they had integrated into the community, as if they had always been here – and yet, not quite. The Waters changed everyone in different ways; we all lost a lot, and it showed. There they were, though, with nothing, and they were as happy as anyone I had ever met. I wanted to give up everything to feel as happy as they felt to me." Jim smiled at both Kaiyo and

Maya and then at Mary, and in that instant Mary felt love for him in a way that she had never felt before.

A lot of heads were nodding in agreement and some people were clapping their hands in appreciation. Jim nodded back at people in acknowledgement and went on.

"I, for one, have restored my faith in humanity and in myself, a gift I am cherishing in every moment. I never thought life could be easy. I never thought I could feel happy for no reason other than being me, and being alive. I can't imagine why I made it so hard before." Jim was in tears and hugged Kaiyo and Maya and Mary, and then just about everyone else in the room. There was a buzz in the room and everyone felt that Jim had spoken for all of them.

Then Mary stood up and stepped forward. "I know that many of you will want Maya, Kaiyo and Hassan to stay, and I also know that, like me, you will want to wish them well on their continuing journey, too," she said as tears came to her eyes again. "I want them to go and show the world what 'being human' means. I want there to be many Whispering Winds. I want everyone to have a place and know what that place is without words, without all the things that get in the way. I want to give them a Whispering Winds send-off and let them know and feel how grateful we are for returning us to ourselves, to each other, and to this beautiful world."

Everyone clapped. "You just did. And we do," said Kaiyo to Mary, and then turned to the room. "We leave in the morning at first light."

Maya's heart took flight at the idea of being at sea with Kaiyo and Hassan and the sun and the sky and the moon and the stars and their open hearts and instincts.

Maya turned to Mary. "I'm going to let Hassan know. I'll be back shortly."

The children were playing in the garden and people had been taking turns to look out for them.

"Hassan," Maya called. "Guess what, sweetheart?"

"Are we going in the morning, Mum?"

She smiled. He already knew. "Yes," she said. "You are your father's son."

"Yours too, Mum," he said and continued to play.

People left quickly so that they could get a good night's sleep and give them a 'Whispering Winds send-off' early the next morning. Hassan fell asleep straight away and Maya and Kaiyo tidied up.

"Everything on the boat is already organised, including your sketching and painting things," said Kaiyo.

"Thank you, darling. I love the way you do that."

"I'll go down to the boat now and see you both in the morning." Kaiyo always preferred to sleep on the boat before a journey, and he went quietly into Hassan's room and kissed him goodnight. "He's sleeping soundly already," he said and kissed Maya. "Sleep well, darling."

"You too," she replied. "We'll catch up with you in the morning."

Maya waved him off and went to bed. She slept her usual sleep before a big adventure; deep, comforting and full of amazing dreams. Hassan also had amazing dreams. He dreamt about swimming with his mum and dad and the sea creatures. He dreamt about playing with them and breathing normally under water for a long time, just like his mum had taught him. He dreamt that the wind whispered in his ears, telling him magical stories and bringing him new tunes.

Kaiyo checked over everything on the boat one more time. He had made the beds and had a special surprise for both Maya and Hassan – a special box for each for the journey. Hassan's box contained his favourite toys and musical instruments. Each was in its own compartment, and was hinged at the side so you could see them all clearly as you opened the box. There was also plenty of room in the bottom for anything else Hassan might want to add. Kaiyo had inscribed the lid with the words The Captain's Box.

Maya's box was a small writing box and he had also inscribed the lid. It read Maya's Imagibox. Just below that, he had carved a beautifully simple carving of Maya and Kiriyu intertwined in an upward twirling dance. Inside, he had put a book that Maya had written since her last journey and illustrations she had started to prepare for it. He had also put in a few essentials, pens, pencils, paints and brushes, along with a small painting palette and paper that Maya had made.

Hassan was up very early the next morning, happy and excited. His father had left him a note to let him know that he had already taken some toys and musical instruments to the boat and that he should bring with him anything else he chose to. Hassan put away a few things in a bag, and was very quiet so as not to wake his mum. He went to the kitchen where she had left him some fruit and cereal for breakfast and ate all the cereal and some of the fruit. After he finished, he pulled a chair up to the window so he could look out to where the boat was moored.

Hassan was an intuitive boy and, like his father, he knew people's hearts. He knew that this was how they connected, and that keeping their hearts open was very important, otherwise they might become ill. Hassan loved to use his music to help people keep their hearts open. It was like magic. His mum said that it was one of his gifts. Gift was a word a bit like 'present' and Hassan liked the word present; so he used his music like a present. It was a present he could give to anyone at any time, and yet he still had it to give to others. That was magic. His mum also said that he had lots of presents that weren't obvious to him and that one day he would find them too. This was amazing because he loved finding presents. His mum helped people to find their presents all the time and he could see that they were happy when they did. He loved his mum.

Hassan looked out of the window and sang softly to himself, "I love my mum fore-v-e-r and e-v-e-r and e-v-e-r."

"What a beautiful present, sweetheart," said Maya who had heard him and walked into the kitchen. "Thank you, and I love you fore-v-e-r."

They both looked out of the window. The light was perfect and they could see the boat in the distance.

"I'll get ready quickly, so we can catch up with Dad on the boat."

"My bag's already packed," said Hassan.

Maya smiled. "Wonderful. How about having a quick shower then? It might be a long day."

Maya had her breakfast while Hassan showered and dressed.

"My turn," she said, as soon as he emerged, and twenty minutes later they were both standing at the front door, ready with their bags.

"Well, sweetheart, this is it," she said, and smiled as they closed the door for the last time.

By the time they had walked down to the beach, everyone had gathered to wish them well. Mary smiled as she saw Maya and put out her arms for Maya to walk right into them. "Go on," Mary said, as she hugged her tightly. "Show us what you're made of."

Maya kissed Mary on both cheeks. "You never know," she said. "I just might."

Many hugs and kisses later, Maya and Hassan set off in their little dinghy to get up to the boat. Maya felt full of life as she saw Kaiyo waving at them and Hassan was still excitedly waving back to everyone on the beach.

As they drew up to the boat, Maya looked up at Kaiyo. "This is it!" she said. "This is the journey that I was always meant to be on, and I'm so grateful that we're all doing it together."

Maya helped Hassan onto the platform at the back of the boat and into Kaiyo's waiting arms.

"Daddy," said Hassan, showering him with kisses.

"Welcome on board, Captain," said Kaiyo.

Hassan smiled. "Can there be two Captains on this boat?"

"There are now," said Kaiyo as he stepped onto the deck and put Hassan down to run around.

Maya stepped onto the platform and turned to tie the dinghy into place. Kaiyo noticed her strong, sure legs and her lean, flexible body. He could make out its outline as the wind caressed her clothes and curled them around her contours. He felt her heart; steadfast, feminine and open. As her hair fluttered in the breeze, he smiled.

"You look amazing," he said. "Radiant like the sun."

Maya turned to look at him. "I am a lucky woman."

"It's not luck, Maya, this is what is meant to be. You and me and Hassan and—"

"And what?" Maya interrupted.

"—and this. All of this," he said and looked up at the sky and closed his eyes in gratitude. "Thank you."

As they stepped onto the deck, Maya picked up Hassan then put an arm around Kaiyo and in that moment she felt complete. "Thank you," she said and gave them both a kiss. "This is perfect."

Maya then turned into the wind and breathed in the air. Kaiyo smiled; Maya seemed to him to be transformed in every moment and in this moment she was a queen, the queen of the sea and of the sky, the queen of the wind and of the water, the queen of all the elements and of the universe.

*This is perfect*, he thought as he too felt complete, and for the first time ever he wondered if he was alive on Earth or had transcended into some world beyond.

"It is, Dad. It always is," said Hassan as Maya put him down to prepare to set sail.

"Darling, which way are we setting off today?" asked Kaiyo.

"I have a feeling that whichever way you choose will instinctively get us to where we are meant to be."

Maya felt this strongly and, although she didn't know where they were going, she knew that she was about to connect pieces of her dreams that she was now beginning to recognise as her past. She wasn't sure how it would happen; she just knew that it would, and that it would be soon. She also knew that this journey would take her there, that she had Kaiyo and Hassan with her and that this was all that mattered.

Maya smelt the air and heard the sounds around her and let them envelop her and seep right into her bones. Kaiyo had set sail and was already standing at the wheel with Hassan in front of him, on a little step that Kaiyo had built so that he could see above the wheel. Kaiyo had his arms around Hassan and his hands on the wheel. Maya looked at them and smiled. *What a pair*, she thought, *so different yet so much the same.*

Apart from his eyes, which were very much like Maya's, Hassan looked like Kaiyo and had a lot of the same facial expressions, especially his smile. Maya loved his smile; it could melt you from a mile away. Hassan's imagination was also very like Maya's; words always conjured up images for him. He also responded to sounds, which he could hear from just about anything. He could then interpret both into music and Maya loved that he could do that; it was a beautiful gift that he shared freely.

Kaiyo felt Maya's warm maternal energy; he was always sensitive to her energy changes and recognised its shifts, particularly when she was with Hassan. He felt that she somehow transferred it to Hassan and that it sustained him – made him grow, even. Kaiyo had learnt about energy transference from Maya and that this was what he did when he was teaching people, for example, carpentry in the boatyard at Whispering Winds. He loved the way she explained it to him; she always seemed to find a way to explain things simply to people, no matter how seemingly improbable they were. He smiled. *I guess that's the reason we've come to be here right now*, he thought.

"That's the reason we've come to be here right now"

Although Kaiyo had always known Maya's heart, he had been a passenger in her world, swept along by her openness, creativity and energy. He had not wanted to leave Whispering Winds, and had felt happy there, until the day that she had disappeared. He knew then that his happiness wasn't to do with a time or a place. Maya had always felt that happiness was an instinct waiting to be felt at any moment, by anyone, whenever they chose. He knew that he could choose to be happy anywhere and he chose to be happy in Maya's world.

As all three stood looking at the horizon and the boat smoothed its way through the water, Hassan's humming resonated inside them all. They were united in all aspects, at one with each other and their environment.

"Maya," said Kaiyo, "I know Kiriyu, and always have done. I'm not sure how I know him; it's kind of always been there inside me."

"Yes," she replied. "You must have done, otherwise how would you have known to put his name on the sign outside my shelter on Ramla?"

"Well, we took it in turns to take care of you before you were strong enough to be up, and you talked in your sleep. You said the name several times, although I feel I knew Kiriyu before then."

"Oh?" Maya looked at Kaiyo for more.

"I'm not sure. He may have rescued me too. It came to me two days ago in my dream, after we'd been swimming."

"Darling, Kiriyu always comes when you're truly connected with the Waters."

"Yes, I know. I feel that there's something more to it than that, though, and that I will know it soon."

"Well, this is the perfect place. Do you remember anything else I talked about?"

"They were words, rather than sentences, and Kiriyu and Maya came up all the time. That's all I remember," he replied, looking apologetic.

She smiled. "Perhaps we'll both remember?"

Maya was right in more ways than she realised. It was the perfect place. Kaiyo put his left arm out and drew her nearer. She leant her head on it and kissed it, just inside the elbow. It sent a beautiful flow of warm energy inside his body. She felt it reach his heart and soothe it. She felt it flow out from his heart and all around the three of them. It was like a fine silk robe flowing in a gentle breeze, its movement and touch calming and healing. Kaiyo felt the energy moving around them, creating a space that seemed out of this world. He felt it all around the boat as if it were protecting them and guiding them on their way. In that moment he knew that this journey was always meant to be and that it was his journey too.

The next morning Maya woke early to keep watch while Kaiyo slept. As she watched the horizon and marvelled at the sky and the sea, she thought of Kiriyu and what Kaiyo had said. She wondered if she might remember him being there too with Kiriyu. She then remembered how Kiriyu had come to save her, and that she had hoped other whales might have saved other people. Then she remembered her mother; she remembered letting go of her hand. She remembered wishing that Malika, Kiriyu's mother, had come to save her own mother.

Maya had remembered her mother! She took a deep breath. She had an image of her now, her long sleek brown hair and how she would twirl it around her finger and tie it up in a bun. She remembered the beautiful pins she used to keep it in place. She remembered wishing that she could do that with her own hair. She remembered how beautiful her mother was. She could see her now, reflected in the mirror as she sat at her dressing table. She remembered a particular dress of hers that she had loved; it was silky and dark red with velvet-encrusted flowers. She remembered seeing a photo of her mother wearing it and looking very much like a film star. She remembered she was wearing a set of pearl earrings and a simple matching string of pearls around her neck. She remembered a white faux-fur stole elegantly poised on her shoulders and how the pearls shone, reflecting her mother's smile. She remembered imagining that her mother was attending a film première, perhaps her own, with photographers at her feet clicking away and asking her to 'Look this way!'.

Maya smiled from deep down inside. Remembering her mother filled her with a sense of belonging. Her heart expanded as if the whole world and all its beings and creatures could easily fit inside. Although Maya knew that she was now distinguishing between her past reality and her dreams and imagination, she had no idea what was yet to come. She closed her eyes and felt the wind in her hair and thought about how amazing it would be to remember how she came to be on Ramla, the day Kaiyo had found her. She wondered if Kaiyo might also have been saved by Kiriyu. Perhaps that's how he had come to be there, and how he knew Kiriyu.

Kaiyo came up from below deck and, as Maya turned to look at him, he kissed her on the nose. "Hello, darling," he said.

"Hello. You didn't sleep much. Did you sleep well?"

"Well? More oddly than well."

"How do you mean, oddly?" asked Maya.

Kaiyo stretched out his arms and let out a yawn. "I had an extraordinary dream and I'm beginning to recognise it as one I've had before, even though I've never remembered it. That's odd, isn't it?"

"I know just what you mean," she said. "Tell me about it."

"Well, I'm swimming in the ocean with other whales—"

Maya interrupted. "Are you a whale?"

"Yes, I am. And you're there too!" he replied.

"I'm a whale too?"

"No," he replied.

"What am I then?"

"You're you and I'm teaching you to be a whale, or rather to be like a whale."

Maya had a vague look on her face as if she was remembering something. "Okay. Then what?"

He shrugged his shoulders. "Then you leave… in a boat."

"I leave in a boat?"

"You leave in a boat," he repeated, and shrugged his shoulders again. "Where did it come from?"

Maya laughed. "You're asking me? It was your dream, darling."

"I know," he replied. "I feel a bit of a novice at this. Perhaps it will become clearer. I have a feeling it will."

Maya was deep in thought. *Kaiyo teaching me to swim?* How extraordinary! She knew that Kaiyo was an incredible teacher and leader, and so was Kiriyu. She remembered how Kiriyu led with amazing ease, despite being one of the youngest whales, and how easily he taught others new skills. Both were also things that could be said of Kaiyo. Maya started to realise that Kaiyo was a lot like Kiriyu – apart from not being a whale, that is. She looked round to see him looking down at the instruments and calculating something. He certainly looked very human and that was as far as she chose to take it.

"Those kind of extraordinary explanations are best left to happen by themselves, that much I know," replied Maya, finally.

Kaiyo smiled at her and nodded in agreement. He was ready to take the helm and Maya was happy to go below to check on Hassan. Hassan had just woken up and was stretching as Maya knocked gently at the door. "Good morning, angel," she said as she put her head around the door.

"Good morning, beautiful Mummy," he said as he stretched his arms to reach around her neck and pull her towards him. "Have we found land yet?"

"Not yet, sweetheart. Would you like to?"

"I think we're going to find it soon," he replied.

"Great, that suits me. And now it's time for breakfast. Let's make some porridge and take it up to Daddy. You know how much he loves that. We'll get you freshened up first, though."

Hassan leapt onto his mother's back. "Mind your head—" she said as she grabbed hold of his legs and ducked down to get out, and again to get into the bathroom, "you might need it later."

Hassan laughed. "You're funny, Mummy."

"I know, sweetheart. It's fun, isn't it?"

Kaiyo could hear lots of giggles and laughter coming from downstairs. *Hassan's definitely up*, he thought. He had been allowing images and feelings from his dream to float around and it wasn't clear to him how or where he and Kiriyu were linked. He looked out at the horizon and chose to allow the explanation to happen by itself when it was ready, as Maya had suggested.

A few minutes later Maya and Hassan came up to the deck with porridge. "Good morning, Captain," said Kaiyo.

"Good morning, Daddy, am I the Captain today?"

"Of course you are," replied Kaiyo as he engaged the wheel latch and picked him up. "Look, you're almost as tall as Daddy."

Hassan put his hand up above his dad's head and stretched himself up. "I'm taller, see?"

"Must be all those oats," Kaiyo replied.

"And here are yours," said Hassan as Maya passed a bowl to Kaiyo. "Better eat them all up, Daddy."

Kaiyo laughed. "I certainly will," and gave Maya a kiss. "Thank you, darling."

Hassan got down and stood on his step to see past the wheel. He flexed his arms to show his muscles. "I can steer the boat all by myself now."

"So you can. Let's see how much breakfast you can eat first, though," said Maya, handing Hassan his bowl and a spoon.

Maya watched Kaiyo and Hassan laughing and sharing breakfast. She wondered what Kaiyo had been like as a child and what his father was like. *I wonder if they laughed and shared like this?* she asked herself.

Hassan ate his breakfast quickly and soon had his hands on the wheel. He loved that feeling. It would resist under his grip and he could feel its energy in his hands and arms and then all over his body.

"Mummy, have you remembered the day the Waters came?" he asked.

"Yes I have. I didn't remember it for a long time though."

"Did you think the water had washed all your memory away?"

"I think I did, sweetheart."

"And now that the water is going back, it's coming back?".

She smiled. "I'd never thought of it like that."

"I wonder what else might come back?" he asked, as if he knew something.

"Me too. I've had lots of memories come back about my mum today," she replied.

"What were they?" asked Kaiyo.

"I remembered how she used to look."

"She was pretty, wasn't she?" Hassan said.

"She was, sweetheart. Can you tell?"

"I saw her, too," he said.

"Did you?" Maya asked, and wondered why she felt surprised by anything Hassan knew. He just seemed to know things – like his dad.

"She was wearing a dress with flowers and pearl earrings and a necklace, and she was sitting by the mirror brushing her hair," Hassan said.

"That's exactly right. She was."

Hassan continued while nodding his head. "And you were looking at her reflection in the mirror from the door so that she couldn't see you."

Maya started nodding too. "That's right, I was supposed to be asleep and didn't want her to know that I was there."

Hassan smiled. "Did you pretend, Mummy?"

"I did, sweetheart, I would pretend to be asleep so that I could go and sneak a look while she was getting ready to go out."

"She told me that she loved you a lot, even though she hadn't told you often, and that she would soon get a chance to tell you herself."

"Okay. I'm not sure how, though," she said, and picked up the empty porridge bowls. She didn't question what Hassan said. She knew that he was very sensitive to her feelings and would often sense her images, sometimes ones she wasn't yet aware of. She went below deck to clear the breakfast things, after which she felt she needed to write and perhaps draw for a while. She walked into the bedroom and opened the wardrobe door to get her Imagibox, and as she closed it saw herself in the mirror. Maya didn't often look at herself in the mirror, even when she was getting dressed. She might take a quick glance occasionally to check that she had her things on straight. She looked again and was amazed at what she saw. It was her childhood room and there was her father coming in. He walked up to her bed and she could see herself as a little girl lying under her princess duvet; she hadn't seen that for a long time.

She had light brown hair, almost fair; it often was in the summer months, as she loved being outside. She smiled a great big smile and her father smiled back. She could see his dark hair, slightly curly as hers was now, and his bright, creative, kind face. He picked up a few of her soft toys that were on a shelf and brought them with him as he positioned the chair close to her bed and sat down.

"Shall we read a story or make one up tonight?" he asked.

"We've never made one up before, Daddy," she said excitedly. "Let's make one up, please."

He settled back into the chair. "Okay. So what's it going to be about?"

Maya remembered everything; she had thought her dad would be the one to make the story up as he had always done. This time, though, he had other ideas and had encouraged her to be the one to make one up. She created her first story with him about a brown bear called Suki, and how when she went to sleep Suki would wake all the other toys up to play. He liked to sing and make the other toys laugh and would dress up and make silly faces. Maya smiled at the thought. She also remembered how her father had suggested that she make some drawings of Suki and the other toys to put in a book. She could see one of those drawings now and Suki's eyes were crooked, almost as if he was winking.

Suki was a bear that her father had bought for her during one of his trips to Japan. His eyes weren't crooked at all, although one of them did eventually get a crack in it. She and her friends used to spend hours dressing him up along with her other soft toys. He had a button on his back, and when she pressed it he would speak in Japanese, which used to make them laugh.

That story about Suki had been her first. Her father had written it out for her and she had made the drawings. Together, they had cut them out and glued them into a scrapbook with pink pages; she could see it now, all frayed at the edges. She had loved doing that with him; it was her very favourite thing, next to being tickled by him, that is.

Maya lay on the bed and closed her eyes. She could see his face clearly now and how handsome he was. She fell asleep and dreamt about him and her mother, about Kaiyo and Kiriyu, about Faye and Angel, and Mary and Jim. It was as if her dreams were putting things in order.

It was already early evening when Maya climbed above deck again. Hassan and Kaiyo looked round at her and smiled as if they knew. No one said a word, and Maya sat down on the deck gazing out at the horizon. Hassan freed himself from under his father's arms at the wheel and climbed into his mother's embrace. He felt her tears and their certainty and clarity; they were creating a space, a wide enormous space, wider than anyone could imagine. Hassan felt their music and started humming.

Maya hugged him. "I can feel it too, sweetheart. I can feel it too."

Kaiyo knelt down beside them, put an arm around each of their shoulders and kissed their heads. He nuzzled up between their damp faces and there they stayed for as long as it took to be – just be. The energy between them was sublime; it was as if they were one person in three bodies. No one needed to say or do anything. The energy swirled around them and the sea, and the skies, and the air. All was healed; all was calm.

The Waters had been calm for several years, as if to make up for being there. The Earth had juddered and vented for many weeks before the oceans had been pushed to the point of no return. None of the earth tremors on their own, or any of the floods they had caused, were significant.

Each earthquake had set off a series of earth tremors and sporadic floods, which eventually synchronised to cause what was undoubtedly the biggest change that had taken place for several centuries. Water levels had risen above all predictions; millions of people had died, and memories and belongings had been lost. For a long time, most did not go near the Waters; they were just there. Now, as the Waters subsided, they left many areas with a welcome rich silty soil. Nutritious plants grew in abundance, and many were heavy with beautifully scented flowers and fruits, the likes of which had not been seen before. The Waters were drawing back to reveal a Heaven on Earth.

By the time the boat neared land Maya, Kaiyo and Hassan had seen several small boats and people fishing and swimming. Maya was particularly delighted to see people swimming. Kaiyo dropped the anchor and, after Maya and Hassan had prepared a few provisions and clothes to take with them, they rowed to shore in their dinghy.

As they neared the shore, they could see sand that stretched for miles. They pulled the dinghy onto it and Maya, as she had done when she first arrived on Ramla, looked down at her feet and watched them sink into the sand and the water swirl around them. It was a lovely feeling. *Maya*, she thought and suddenly knew the reason why.

They all felt a little giddy, and Hassan lurched around a bit. "Mummy, I feel odd, like the ground is moving,"

"Yes, me too, sweetheart, that happens when you've been on the water for a while and then you go on to land. It'll soon disappear when you get used to the feel of the ground again."

Kaiyo and Maya looked at each other as they took the few things they had brought with them out of the dinghy.

"Well, we're here," said Kaiyo.

"So we are," replied Maya. "And do you know what? *Maya* is the Arabic word for water. That's how I got my name. It was the first thing that came to me when I got to Ramla all those years ago."

"I always knew that Maya wasn't what you were called before, just as Angel wasn't Angel," replied Kaiyo.

"So do you know what I was called before?"

"Well, the day we met… well, not exactly met. I just saw you from a distance—"

Maya interrupted. "Do you mean on the beach at Ramla?"

"I mean at the Wadi," said Kaiyo.

"Wadi El-Hitan?" asked Maya, surprised first at the idea that they'd met before Ramla, then at remembering the Wadi and its name.

"I think you were with your mother and a man. Not your dad, I guess."

"Hassan!" she said, making the connection with the name and smiling at Hassan.

"Hassan, of course. The guide! Great guy," replied Kaiyo.

"You knew him?"

"Not really. I knew of him. I wasn't taking much notice of who was with you, though. I was busy looking at you."

"What? I was only thirteen!"

"Thirteen! You must be joking. You looked at least sixteen or seventeen!"

Maya smiled. "I know, it's my long legs," she said, cheekily pulling up one of her trouser legs to show one off.

"I'll tell you everything I know tonight," replied Kaiyo.

"Everything you know about what?" she asked.

"I think I've somehow always known that I knew you before Ramla, Maya. I just didn't know how, till early this morning – and even then I wasn't sure till a moment ago. All I know and all I've always known is that I was hooked from the moment I saw you in the Wadi. And Ramla. And…" he shrugged his shoulders and smiled, "…well, every day really."

"I'm looking forward to finding out what everything you know is, then," she said. "First, let's concentrate on finding a place to stay," and she smiled at the thought of Kaiyo knowing her *before* Ramla. She bent down, gave Hassan a kiss and helped him with his bag before picking up her own. "I'm also looking forward to this adventure, and I can hardly wait to meet our new friends."

Hassan was excited. "Me too, Mum," he said. "I'm going to get together with them to play music."

"Great idea," said Kaiyo as he secured the dinghy to a jetty. "We'll do a concert in the Wadi."

"Is that where the whales were?" asked Hassan. "I wonder what happened to them, and all the other sea creatures."

"Let's go and find out," said Kaiyo. "Darling, I'd love to go straight to the Wadi. Do you think we might be anywhere near?"

"Of course," she said. "The Wadi – *that's* what we're here for!"

# CHAPTER SEVEN

# Wadi I

Maya, Kaiyo and Hassan walked hand in hand across the sand towards a road on the other side of the beach. They could see a group of people standing next to a minibus, and Kaiyo walked up to them. He asked if they knew Wadi El-Hitan and how to get there.

One of them pointed up a hill at another minibus. It belonged to a friend of his, who was on his way to a small airfield a couple of hours away. "He might be able to help you," he said. "I know he used to fly there regularly."

Before long they were on their way to the small airfield. The man who owned the minibus was on his way there to fly down to what he called the southern coast. He said that he had stopped going to the Wadi several months ago, and he knew someone who went there regularly, who may be able to take them.

"Wow, Dad, are we going to fly?"

It hadn't occurred to Kaiyo that this would be Hassan's first time in a plane. "We certainly are, and you will love it!" he replied.

Hassan looked at his mother and could barely contain his excitement. She smiled at him. "I remember my first time, sweetheart. I was so excited and I loved it, especially taking off – that's the moment the plane leaves the ground."

Hassan was even more excited now. "Did it feel like it was you who was flying?"

"Exactly," she replied. "Only with a jet engine to help."

"There's quite a community out there now," said the man. "It's a totally different place to how it used to be."

"What kind of community?" asked Maya.

"Oh, scientists and journalists and photographers and travellers," he replied.

"What do you mean, travellers?" she asked.

"Some were, you know, people who were there when the floods came and found their way back there. Others travelled there because they felt it was a significant place, you know, given that it was a sea a long time ago."

Maya nodded. "Yes, I know."

"Is that why you're going?" the man asked.

"Well, I was there—"

The man interrupted. "When the floods came? Sorry. I interrupted—"

"That's okay. And, yes, I was there when the floods came."

"That must have been quite a thing. I'll be quiet now."

A hot and slightly sticky two hours later, they were driving through a very small town and shortly afterwards arrived at the airfield. There were a few light planes on the ground and one was taxiing down the short runway, about to take off.

Hassan looked in amazement. "Whoever came up with that idea was very clever."

"You're right there, very clever," the man confirmed to Hassan, then looked at Kaiyo and Maya. "If you wait here, I'll go and talk to my friend and see if I can negotiate you a ride."

A few minutes later they were at the foot of the steps of a private plane. Kaiyo turned to the man who had given them the lift and shook his hand. "Thank you," he said. "We appreciate your help."

"My pleasure. I was coming down here anyway and, as it happens, my friend is on his way to the Wadi to pick up some passengers."

He turned to Maya. "I hope you find what you're looking for there."

Maya smiled. "Thank you. That's very kind of you."

"All in a day's work," he replied and waved them off.

They were greeted at the top of the aircraft steps by the pilot. "I'm Richard," he said, "and I'm at your service." He shook Kaiyo's hand, then Maya's and then Hassan's. "I understand it's your first time."

"Yes," replied Hassan as he stepped into the plane. He looked to the left and could see where the pilot sat, along with lots of dials and switches.

"Well, welcome on board," said Richard.

"Thank you," Hassan replied, noticing that there were eight seats. He hoped that no one else was coming, and imagined himself flying his mum and dad in his own plane. He sat down next to a window, fastened his seatbelt, and closed his eyes. So, there he was in his very own plane swooping down to the sea and he could see all the sea creatures and they could see him. It was a beautiful sunny day and the sea sparkled.

"Hassan," said Maya. "Are you asleep already?"

"No, I was imagining, Mum."

"Oh, sorry to have interrupted. I was wondering if you would like to go up front?"

"Up front where the pilot is?" His heart skipped a beat.

"Yes. Off you go," she said. "Dad will show you." Maya smiled; she knew Hassan well and was sure that whatever he was imagining had something to do with him flying a plane.

Hassan, like his dad, knew exactly what to do, even in situations he'd never been in before. He walked into the cockpit and sat in the co-pilot's chair, strapping himself in.

"Hello again," said Richard. "I understand you'd like to be a pilot. Would you like to help me fly the plane?"

Hassan gave him a big smile. "Yes please!"

He sat tall in the co-pilot's chair and listened and watched the pilot with total concentration as he prepared for takeoff. "I can see you're a clever young man; seems like you're going to make a great pilot one day."

"And a sailor," replied Hassan. "I love both."

"Well, the sea and the sky have a lot in common. Let's just concentrate on one for now, to make sure we get there safely."

"I'll see you later then, Hassan," said Kaiyo as he turned to join Maya.

"Yes. Thanks, Dad," and he turned to the pilot. "Do you know the Wadi, where we're going?"

"Sure, I used to go there daily. It's not quite the same any more though. There's nothing left of the skeletons."

Hassan interrupted, "My mum's seen them. She was there before the flood."

"So I understand. Right, are you ready for take-off?" asked Richard, and Hassan was.

Hassan helped the pilot complete his checks and watched in fascination as he started the engine. It roared into action, then the pilot moved the plane forward gently to start the short taxi down the runway. It felt bumpy to start with then, as they joined the main runway, they quickly accelerated away.

"Woohoo," shouted Hassan and everyone heard him. "This is amazing!"

Hassan had always loved sailing and thought it was the most amazing experience learning to handle the boat, navigating and feeling the tug of the water and the waves. He never imagined that anything could come close. He had floated and flown in his dreams many times; and now, here he was experiencing flying in a plane and it was wonderful.

As the plane gently climbed, Hassan could see the ground below just as he saw it in his dreams. The plane then circled round to the right and he could see the small airfield and runway that they had just taken off from. Things on the ground looked smaller and smaller until they totally disappeared. The desert unfolded, in beautiful contrast to the sky ahead, and far in the distance they blended in a shimmering haze.

Kaiyo and Maya sat together and held hands. The next stage of their journey was going to be significant, and neither knew quite how much. Maya thought about them choosing to go back to the Wadi. Going back was something neither of them usually did, at least not since the floods, and it was highly unlikely that anything remained. She suddenly felt tears in her eyes as she remembered how her mother had read her the article about the discovery of the whale skeletons, and the Wadi becoming a UNESCO World Heritage site. She remembered feeling close to her for the first time, after what seemed like an age since her father had died. She felt close to her now, and smiled.

Kaiyo was smiling too; he was looking ahead at the terrain and felt he recognised some of it, despite the changes. As he looked at the mountain outlines, he remembered crossing this part of the desert in a jeep with a couple of journalists.

He laughed as he realised. "I was a journalist," he said.

"You were?" asked Maya, already knowing the answer. "That might explain why you were at the Wadi."

Kaiyo's smile broadened – he also remembered saying that he should have picked an easier life and been a carpenter or a cabinet-maker like his dad. That was the first time he had remembered his dad. He remembered his greying hair and his wide sideburns that made him look like something out of a history book. He remembered how he would dance around him and play silly games while his dad was making him something to play with.

"Dad was a carpenter," he said. "It's all coming back now."

"Really? That's amazing! You're a chip off the old block, then?" Maya smiled.

"Dad used to make me toy boats. I had hundreds of them! He used to make them from all sorts of leftover wood. They were works of art. They had working parts. They were spectacular!" He smiled. "Yes, sorry, a chip off the old block indeed."

"It's all connected, isn't it? I mean, the past and the present," replied Maya. "I thought that somehow the Waters had cut that connection and that we had started totally new lives."

"We did, Maya. Life was very different on Ramla. People were different."

Maya smiled as she remembered Faye and Angel and the weaving and the dyeing. "Yes, it was, and they were. We were so close to the land and everything just flowed."

"I used to be a journalist!" Kaiyo said again, distracting Maya from her thoughts of Ramla.

"Yes, I know! Nothing to do with being a carpenter or building boats, and yet that's what you chose to do in this life."

"This life?" said Kaiyo. "That's exactly what it feels like – another life. Who knows what's going to happen next?" He picked up her hand and caressed it gently in both of his. "Darling, you have a way of saying things that is quite extraordinarily accurate. You always manage to put into words exactly how I feel or what I'm thinking. Do you know how wonderful that is?"

Maya, reached up and kissed Kaiyo on the forehead and whispered, "I love you too, darling, and have always known how extraordinary you are. Extraordinarily talented, extraordinarily connective, extraordinary at learning and teaching, extraordinary at making things, especially out of wood."

Hassan came into the cabin to join them and sat on his dad's lap. "That was amazing, Dad."

"We knew you'd love it," Kaiyo replied.

"I mean about you remembering being a journalist and your dad making boats."

"Ah yes, that. I used to come out here all the time. I would fly or go by jeep to get to the Wadi, and looking out of the window helped me to remember."

Hassan looked out of the window and imagined his father in a jeep, tracking the plane from the ground. He imagined him with a camera in his hand, standing up out of his seat and taking a photo of the plane. His shirt was open and it fluttered in the breeze. Underneath it, he wore a T-shirt with an unusual blue and white illustration with swirls and dots.

Hassan was suddenly aware of a change in the engine noise, and realised that they were nearing the ground. He looked out of the window and could see three cars below on a stretch of road. The cars seemed to be racing to meet the plane and he thought he could see someone waving.

"Hassan," said Maya, "we'll be landing shortly. Sit in this seat next to Dad and put your seatbelt on. I'll be just over there."

Hassan sat down and put his seatbelt on, then did his best to stretch forward to see if the cars were still there. Then he heard a noise coming from somewhere under his feet.

"That's the wheels dropping down, ready for touchdown," said Kaiyo loudly, so that Hassan could hear him, since the engine was now pretty loud too. Hassan smiled. He could tell that he would love landing as much as he had taking off.

"Look, there are those cars again, Dad."

Kaiyo didn't quite hear him over the engine noise, although he knew that he had said something to do with the cars, and he nodded at him in acknowledgment then sat back and closed his eyes. Maya was sitting back too with her eyes closed; she was opening her heart to whatever was going to happen. No expectations, no desires, just whatever there was. Sometimes the way we want things to *be* gets in the way of the way things *are*. She needed to be present, since so much past and so much future could be about to come together. No matter what happened, she knew it was down to her to choose how to be.

Hassan put a gentle hand on his mother's shoulder. "Wake up, Mum, we need to get out of the plane!"

"Thank you, sweetheart," she replied and unbuckled her belt.

The pilot opened the door of the plane and, as she reached for her bag, she heard men shouting: "Steve, you old bastard, what the hell took you so long? We've been waiting for you forever!"

*I wonder who Steve is*, she thought as she turned, and realised that they were talking to Kaiyo. He was being hugged by three men who seemed to know him well. Kaiyo's initial look of bemusement turned into joyous recognition.

"My God, don't you guys have anything better to do?" he replied.

As Kaiyo was being bundled out of the plane by his friends, Hassan looked at his mum. "Mum?" he said. "I think those men were in the cars I saw earlier. I think they were racing to catch up with us. One of them had a T-shirt on just like the one that Dad had."

"Which T-shirt, sweetheart?"

"It was one I saw in my imagination and it had a blue and white sign on. I think he used to wear it before. I mean before in the past."

"Yes, I know what you mean, sweetheart," she said. "Let's go and find out."

Maya and Hassan came out of the plane and down the steps. They could see Kaiyo with a circle of people around him, and Hassan could see the cars he had seen earlier, racing to meet the plane. As they approached, the circle opened and Kaiyo said, "And this is my wife, Maya, and my son, Hassan."

Hassan ran up to his father and leapt up to hug him, almost knocking him over. "I'm getting too big for you now, Dad."

"Quite the little man," said one of the men who had come to the plane to meet Kaiyo.

Kaiyo put out his arm and held Maya at his side.

"My God, you look the spit of Josie," said a woman who came forward in the crowd.

"Who's Josie?" asked Maya.

"Who isn't Josie?" replied the woman. "You might like to find out for yourself."

"Yes, please. I would like to. Where is she? How far is it?"

"It's not far," replied the woman. "It's where we're going anyway. It's about an hour's drive, although it could be faster."

The woman turned and asked one of the men if they could swap cars and go with him, since he had a faster car. She turned to the man she had come with and said, "Sorry," and gestured to Maya, Kaiyo and Hassan to get into a large white car. She climbed into the front. "I'm Beka," she said, once they were all in.

"And I'm Maya," responded Maya. "And thank you for taking us to meet Josie." Maya knew in her heart who Josie was although she didn't recognise the name.

"I'm Mark," said the man. "Steve and I used to work together."

"Are you a journalist?" asked Maya.

"Blimey, is it that obvious?" replied Mark. "I did once think about giving it up to do something else. It didn't last for long, though."

"What did you do instead?" she asked.

He smiled and shrugged his shoulders. "Mostly contemplated my navel."

"And what did you want to do?"

"Be a musician," he replied, and Hassan's ears pricked up. "It just wasn't going to happen, though."

"What stopped you?"

"Oh, mostly me," he said shaking his head. "Me, myself and I have always had that kind of relationship. I want to do something and I find all sorts of reasons why not to do it."

"I know exactly what you mean," replied Maya. "It's easy to find reasons not to do things when we're fearful of what might be the result."

Mark looked a little surprised and wondered why he would be fearful of the result. He was quiet for the rest of the journey and so was everyone else. He allowed himself to be with what Maya had said.

The sun was low in the sky when they finally arrived at a few huts and makeshift buildings set in a vague semicircle. There were a few people buzzing about and two were lighting a fire away from the buildings. Beka got out of the car, gestured for them to wait, and disappeared into the second hut.

Mark turned to Maya. "Finding out that I might actually be very bad at something that I so much want to be good at is a scary proposition. I'd put it down to being burnt-out and overworked; turns out it was just a convenient excuse. Thank you."

Maya smiled and nodded. "You're welcome. It's taken me a long time to get here and I too was fearful of what might be the result. And still am," she said as she saw Beka and another woman coming out of the hut and hurrying towards them

"It's a good job you arrived when you did," said the other woman.

Maya was transfixed. *How—?* she thought as something in her had her open the car door and leap out of it almost at the same time.

Kaiyo and Hassan looked on in amazement and knew. Maya was locked in a long, loving, healing embrace with Josie, or Josephine, as she now remembered her mother's name to be. Tears were rolling down both their faces; they had gone through disbelief and relief to joy, which soon turned into laughter.

"I always knew, darling, that you would come back, and that I had to be here when you did." Josie looked at Maya, who nodded. "I felt you always, especially when you had Hassan. Remember our driver, Hassan?"

"Yes," smiled Maya as she looked at Hassan. "I remember."

"He somehow got me to safety," continued Josie. "I've no idea how; I was sure I had died."

"Me too, Mum – I mean, I was sure I had died," she smiled again. "I thought Malika might have come to save you."

"It was definitely Hassan, darling, and some help from above, perhaps."

Maya continued, "I had no idea what had gone before, just fragmented images. I had no idea who I was or how I came to be there – except for Kiriyu, that is."

"Kiriyu?" replied Josie. "That was when it happened."

"When what happened?"

"A whole lifetime, darling," Josie replied, shaking her head. "A whole lifetime, and we'll soon catch up with it all. Let's get you all in, fed and settled. It gets dark around here very quickly."

Beka had already shown Kaiyo and Hassan to the building near where the fire had been lit.

"This is where we all sleep," she said. "It's cosy and we all get along pretty well most of the time."

She saw someone coming in, and they nodded to each other and smiled.

"If you're okay to sleep here tonight," she continued, "we'll find you a space together in the morning."

Maya walked in with Josie, and Hassan ran over to greet them.

"Hello, my darling Hassan," said Josie, "you won't believe how much I was looking forward to seeing you."

"Me too," he replied.

Josie turned to Kaiyo. "So you're the man who stole my daughter's heart."

"Well—" started Kaiyo.

"Enough said," Josie interrupted and they all started laughing.

Maya looked at her mother as she laughed. *Still beautiful,* she thought, *and so vibrant, so alive, so … happy to be with her.* Maya's heart filled and expanded and somehow she felt Faye talking to her. "You found her," she said, smiling. "I knew you would." *I did*, Maya replied in her imagination, and put out her hand to touch her mother. She sighed, *I definitely did.*

Maya saw her mother in the beautiful dress with the velvet-encrusted flowers that she had loved from her childhood. Her hair was up in a bun and it shone, as did her eyes and the beautiful pair of pearl earrings dangling from her ears. As her mother stood there speaking to Hassan and Kaiyo, she watched her mouth move as she used to do with her father, content to be by her side.

Maya slept happily that night, looking forward to connecting and being with her mother. She felt a deep sense of joy and wholeness. She had lived with no past for most of her life except for the dreams and images in her subconscious. Eventually they had helped her create a link to her conscious and led her here. She recognised the need for the subconscious to be complete and she loved that it had helped her realise a dream that she might never have felt was possible.

Maya woke early; she wanted to eat breakfast with her mother, who had also woken early. Maya showered and dried herself quickly then almost fell over while she hopped around, attempting to put her trousers on with one hand and clean her teeth with the other. She couldn't wait to share with her mother the adventures that she'd had and the people she had met on the way. She wanted to tell her about Faye and Ramla and how free the people were there, except that they didn't like to go in the water. She wanted to tell her about Kaiyo, and the bed he had built her from the boat and the dried grasses. She wanted to tell her how she came to be here.

Maya looked out of the window and saw her mother waving to her to join her. She put on her socks and picked up her shoes to put them on outside so she didn't wake anyone. She quickly slipped them on and ran up to her mother and kissed her.

"Good morning, darling," her mother whispered. "Let's go for a picnic."

Maya was excited. "A picnic! Yes please."

Her mother smiled. "No time like the present."

"Present," said Maya. "I've always loved that word."

Josie led Maya up a mountain pass to a beautiful plain full of young grass-like plants and beautiful yellow flowers. Maya bent down to look at them. They looked so fragile and paper-like and yet, there they were, filling up the earth with their beauty.

"I love this colour, Mum," she said.

"I know, darling. That's why we're here."

Josie found a spot at the edge of the plain by a tree and laid down a blanket for them to sit on. She had brought a picnic breakfast.

Maya couldn't believe what was coming out of her mother's bag. All sorts of breads and jams and cheeses and fruit and, and, and …

"Wow, Mum! When did you make all this?"

"I've been busy. And look at this," she said as she held up a fruit.

"A mango!" exclaimed Maya in delight. "That's one of my all-time favourites!" and they both laughed, remembering that the first time she had drunk mango juice she had said the same thing.

The two women ate their breakfast, sharing smiles and laughter without saying very much. It had been a lifetime and yet now it felt as if it had been no time at all.

"Mum, what was my name before now – I mean, before the Waters?" asked Maya as they were clearing up.

"Do you know what, darling? I don't remember. It's as if it's been wiped away. Is it very important to you?"

Maya shook her head. "Not important, just interesting. Kaiyo's was Steve."

"Kaiyo is a lovely name. Do you use a name now?"

"Maya," she replied with a smile.

"Spot on," said Josie, smiling back. "It's beautiful."

"Can you remember Dad's name?"

Josie shook her head slightly. "It might have been Mark, or Max, I'm not certain. Both names have come up for me occasionally."

"Okay," replied Maya.

"Darling, has me not remembering your name upset you?"

"Yes. It's a strange feeling."

"I was upset about it for a long time too. I'm sorry."

Maya held Josie's hand and stroked it. "When I first arrived on Ramla – that's the name I chose for it, by the way—" explained Maya.

"You always did like choosing names for things," said Josie.

"Yes, I remember that now. Well, Kaiyo tells me I was slumped over the back of a boat, and I thought Kiriyu had saved me."

"Kiriyu?" Her mother was puzzled.

"Maybe he did... then somehow turned into a boat." Maya smiled as she attempted to explain.

"Mum, do you know what? It's not important. What's important is now."

"Spot on again," said Josie. "Spot on."

As Maya and Josie walked back to the camp, Maya enjoyed the beautiful scene surrounding her. It was so different to how the Wadi was before. It was full of a different yellow now; the pale yellowness of the flowers.

"It's only ever about now," she said and filled her lungs with air. She felt them opening wide and her heart filling with joy and soaring to the sun and beyond.

"A plane!" she said.

"Yes," said Josie. "We have the usual visitors. Let's go and catch up with Hassan and Kaiyo first, though."

Kaiyo and Hassan were up on ladders, busy helping to repair one of the buildings. It had been built in a hurry and the roof structure wasn't holding up too well. It had been one of the sleeping quarters

Picnic at the Wadi

until the last time it had rained, and a few people woke up to find themselves, and their beds, very wet. Kaiyo saw them approach.

"Good morning, darling, and good morning, Josie."

"Good morning, Mum," smiled Hassan.

"Good morning!" replied Maya and her mother in the same breath.

Maya looked at her mother. "Kaiyo's great at this kind of thing, fixing roofs, I mean. Actually, fixing anything."

"Wonderful!" said Josie. "That'll be very welcome around here."

"Hassan enjoys it too, although his thing is music."

"Really, darling, that makes two of us. Does he play an instrument?"

"He plays them all, Mum, and makes them too. I think he can make music from just about anything."

Josie smiled. "A man after my own heart," she said and shouted up to Hassan. "Hello, young man."

"Hello," replied Hassan. "Can we make some music after we've finished fixing this roof?"

"We most certainly can. What do you like to play?"

"Something with a round sound," he said.

"I think I might have the very thing. Just you finish what you're doing first."

Hassan nodded in response. "I will."

The community at the Wadi had grown after the floods had subsided, with many people returning to see if there was anything left of the skeletons. None remained, nor did much of anything else. All the buildings had been swept away, and much of the desert had turned into savannah. Just like many other areas around the world, new flowers and plants had appeared, and the Wadi was particularly abundant. Many people had turned up to study the flora, and believed there was something special about the Wadi, as well as its part in the floods. They also believed that these new plants and flowers needed analysis and categorisation. They believed that the plants could reveal something about the floods; many others couldn't see the point, Josie included.

Josie felt that the plants and flowers were just there, and it didn't matter how or why. She wondered why we needed to know so much about the past or even predict the future; none of it had stopped the floods. Things just were and always will be, and it was no use studying them in the pretence that we can be in control. We spend our whole lives wanting and attempting to be in control of someone or something, and yet we never truly are.

# CHAPTER EIGHT

# Josie's Journey

When the Waters came, Josie had been swept off to the east and ended up beached in an area between the Sahara Desert and the Red Sea, along with a few other people. She sometimes wondered why her daughter hadn't ended up there too. For a while it would have been easy to believe that she must have died and to let go of her. She certainly had a lot to occupy her – like staying alive. One of the reasons that she hadn't let go was that she simply could not remember her name. For a while she couldn't remember her own name, and that was frustrating enough. Not remembering her daughter's name felt like she had a lead weight in her heart.

Josie would wake up tearful most mornings, struggling to survive and be present to anyone or anything. She didn't know what to say or how to be. She would sit there and smile, no matter what was happening around her, until one day she couldn't stand it any longer. She stood up, dusted herself off, and announced that she was going back to the Wadi, even though she had no idea how. To her astonishment, others chose to join her, some who had never been there before, feeling drawn to her sense of purpose.

Josie's journey took many years; she surprised herself with her resourcefulness and ingenuity. She walked long distances and took great care of the people who came with her. Initially there was Josie, five other women and a man. It was through conversations with one of the women, about forgetting people's names, that she had remembered her own. Actually, she wasn't sure it was her name; it came to her clearly and she identified with it, so that was who she chose to be. It gave her a renewed sense of herself, and a stronger sense of her daughter.

Josie's journey was one of transformation, as well as purpose and distance. She emerged as the natural leader of the group, and often caught herself saying and doing things that seemed to her as if someone else was saying and doing them. Eventually, she became at ease with the emerging woman whom she now accepted as herself. She felt a sense of deep satisfaction and happiness that she had never experienced before, and she loved every minute of it.

When she eventually arrived at the Wadi, it was full of yellow flowers; she remembered her daughter's love of the colour. Every day she was there, the feeling that she would see her daughter again strengthened, although it would be several years before it happened. She woke up each morning with a sense of her daughter being close to her. She had images of her all the time and felt she knew what her daughter was doing at significant times. She felt she knew about Kaiyo and her first adventure across the Waters, to what became Healing Waters. She felt she knew about Hassan's arrival and when her daughter finally chose to come and find the Wadi – and her.

Josie became the *de facto* leader of the community at the Wadi, which was by now full of people from all over the world. Apart from the scientists, who had come to categorise everything, there were the 'story tellers' and the 'story makers', as Josie called them. Story tellers were people who came to observe and tell it like it is. Story makers were people who already knew their story, and came to find evidence for it. Josie didn't have much time for the story makers.

There were also people, like Josie, who had been there when the floods came and had come back to connect with someone, or something. Mostly, though, the people there weren't sure why they had come; they had just felt drawn to it. Both the latter groups were referred to as travellers and – no matter who they were – everyone knew Josie and Josie knew them.

Beka had arrived at the Wadi before Josie. She was a journalist and had been sent, along with a cameraman, on a project to film and report on what the scientists and the travellers were doing. Josie connected with Beka straight away and liked that she saw things as they were, no matter what anyone wanted her to see. Beka worked for an organisation which, by her own description, 'traded in stories'. Josie wondered how they had the time, or the inclination. Josie and Beka would often talk about people's level of curiosity about other people's lives and why journalists came to investigate and report on them.

"Are people really so curious, or do they need to fill their time with something?" Josie would ask. "They should get up and find out for themselves if it's so important to them, instead of busying themselves with other things and having other people doing the finding out for them." It seemed to her that being concerned with other people's business, rather than with getting to know them, was a little strange.

Beka felt that it was a throwback from the past. "I think it comes from a need to be sure that others aren't a threat, or out to harm you."

"I can understand that," Josie would say. "It's time to give it all up, though. We've all been through a lot, and going back to doing the same things all over again is just asking for trouble."

Beka agreed. "It took a flood to create an amazing new world on this Earth and it will take each one of us to keep on creating new worlds and new ways of being and doing and feeling, rather than going back to the old ways."

Josie was ready for a new journey, to make a difference in this new world and to have it continue to create an amazing future. Her intention was to take her daughter and her family and Beka with her, if they would come. The day that Maya returned was perfect; more people had arrived the day before and Josie felt the urge to go on with her journey. She had woken up feeling energised, with a new sense of freedom.

"This is the day!" she had said, so loudly that several people heard her.

Beka rushed in to see what was happening, her hair dripping wet. "What's going on? I was in the middle of washing my hair!"

"Then you'd better hurry up and finish before you cause another flood," Josie replied. "You need to get yourself down to the airfield double-quick, young woman. I have a feeling that today will be the day that my daughter comes back."

"I see," Beka replied and couldn't think what else to say.

"Beka," Josie said in a soft voice, "I need you to go and meet our guests and I need to stay here and prepare for their arrival. It's important."

"Of course," Beka said and hurried back to the bathroom to get ready, letting the cameraman know on the way that he should be ready to come with her in five minutes.

The cameraman was always ready; he had checked his camera and sat in the driver's seat for a laugh while he was waiting for her. To his surprise, when Beka came out, she said nothing and simply sat in the passenger seat. She usually preferred to drive. She looked at him and he knew straight away that this was an important meeting. They drove quickly and, before they knew it, a couple of cars with other journalists were following, presumably thinking that they were up to something interesting that they wanted to be part of.

It was a clear morning and the sun was throwing a gentle pale light onto the desert sands and mountains. Beka loved the soft warmth and often woke early to enjoy it and have time to herself. That morning was very different; she felt a togetherness that gave her a depth of being that was new to her. She was looking forward to meeting Josie's daughter, although she wondered if this would be the day that she would arrive.

Beka felt excited and, unusually, allowed herself to express it. As they tracked through the desert, she breathed deeply and stood up, letting the wind catch her hair. The cameraman looked at her. He had always felt that there was something special about her and, for the first time, felt a bond with her and wondered if she was feeling something similar. She had closed her eyes and, as he saw her profile, her forehead, her nose, her cheeks and her mouth, he smiled.

"Keep your eyes on the road, Mr Cameraman," she said.

"Of course, your Highness," he replied, smiling even more because he had seen her smiling too.

Beka had been a writer all her life, and came to journalism after the floods. Before that she had written crime thrillers; she wasn't sure why she had chosen that subject, other than she liked the idea of investigating things to uncover the truth. She made her home in Switzerland in an area close to the border with Italy, because she loved the mountains. Her mother was Italian and her father French–Swiss and Beka could speak all three languages well. She had been an interpreter in the European Parliament in Brussels and, after both her parents died in a car accident, she moved closer to where her mother was born.

Beka enjoyed being a writer, although it was a solitary occupation and nothing like her job in Brussels. Her books didn't sell well, and while she never let it bother her too much, she always felt that something was missing from her life. After the floods, despite the fact that where she lived had not been affected, she made the choice to travel to the Wadi. On the way there, she met the editor of a French travel magazine. He told her that he wanted to publish a new type of journal, one about how people's lives changed after the floods. After a little negotiation, she agreed to do some work for him. Everything was fine until she found out that she needed to travel with a cameraman; her idea had been to travel on her own.

Beka had never asked Mr Cameraman his name, and he had never offered it. *I'll ask him when we get to the airfield*, she thought. *It's too noisy now*. As they approached the airfield she saw a plane in the distance.

"Gosh, we'd better get a move on," she said, "or we'll miss the arrival!"

Mr Cameraman nodded and gestured to her to sit down and waited until she did so before accelerating away. She liked that he did that. Soon the cars behind them overtook them, and it became a bit of a friendly race.

"Sorry," he said, "this jeep's not very fast." The driver and passenger of one of the other cars waved to them as they drove past.

"We used to work together," he explained.

They arrived at the airfield just as the plane was drawing to a standstill. As soon as it dropped its steps, the two men who had waved to Mr Cameraman earlier jumped out of the car and hurried towards them. Mr Cameraman suddenly seemed to know why, and ran up behind them.

Beka sat still for a while, watching, and wondering what had happened to make Mr Cameraman so animated. She watched as they came out with one of the passengers from the plane. *Clearly a very important person*, she thought. *It's not like him to leave his camera behind.* Then she grabbed the camera and started clicking away. That's when she saw Maya and Hassan emerge. *My God! Is that who I think it is?* She had jumped out of the car and took the camera with her. If Beka had had any doubt up until then, all was removed in that second. Maya looked like a younger version of Josie. *So, this is the day after all*, she thought as she put away the camera. It somehow seemed appropriate.

# CHAPTER NINE

# Wadi II

The roof repairs were finished, the sun was dipping below the horizon and the whole camp had a warm glow about it. Josie had posted notes on everyone's doors requesting anyone with a musical instrument to bring them out after dinner to play together. There was an excited hum around the camp, and many people chose to have dinner earlier than usual. Some had already lit fires to cook outside. Areas had been designated specifically for this, and everyone respected them. They also became natural social areas, ideal for any gathering.

Dinner was over quickly and everyone was looking forward to a night of music. The handful of people who brought instruments were tuning them and practising while waiting for Josie. Josie was still inside, clearing up after dinner with her little family, which now included Beka and Mr Cameraman.

"Josie, you're an amazing cook," said Mr Cameraman as he helped with the dishes.

"Well, thank you. I always like to keep things simple."

"I've never been quite sure how to cook these. Please tell me your secret," he asked, as he looked at the selection of vegetables in her kitchen.

Josie was pleased to be asked. "Well, the secret's in the combination. You don't actually have to cook them at all."

"Ah, that's why your kitchen is so clean. You should see mine when I attempt to cook!"

"Mine, too," said Beka.

Maya and Kaiyo looked at each other, then at Hassan. Maya looked at Beka and smiled. There was something about her that was familiar, and she was happy that she was bonding beautifully with Mr Cameraman.

"That was just amazing, Mum. You certainly know how to pick your ingredients."

"It's easy when you grow them yourself," replied Josie. "I'll show you tomorrow if you like."

"Yes, I would like that," said Maya.

"Me too," said Hassan.

Maya smiled at Hassan then continued. "Then I can tell you all about Faye. I would love you to meet her; she certainly knows her plants."

Josie turned to Maya. "Maya, I'd love it if we could travel together."

"That would be perfect, Mum" said Maya and looked at Kaiyo and Hassan, who both nodded.

"Great, that's settled then," replied Josie. "We can talk about it tomorrow. Now all I want to do is to listen to and play some music. What do you think, Hassan?" Hassan had a mouthful of fruit and nodded excitedly.

"No reply needed," said Kaiyo.

Josie walked round the table to Hassan. "Come with me, young man. I have a little surprise for you," she said, walking to the other end of the hut. Hassan left the table and skipped past his parents with a big smile on his face, then ran off to catch up with Josie.

"These are all instruments that I have made, Hassan," she said opening a box she'd made to put them in. "I have always felt that there was another reason why I had made them. It would be lovely if you would play them." She picked out a couple to show him.

Hassan looked at the instruments with wonder; they were beautifully made, "Josie," he said, holding one up, "I would love to play this one tonight." Hassan picked up a wide flute-like instrument that Josie had barely played.

"Then it's yours to keep – and tonight let's play them all!"

Josie put the instruments back in their box so that they could be carried out easily. "I can help," said Hassan, and held the handle on one side.

Josie smiled and held the other. "Let's go, then. We're keeping people waiting."

"When we see what instruments everyone else has, Josie, then we can choose which to play first."

"Fabulous idea. Let's do that."

The two of them picked up the box and walked back into the room where the others were.

"Time to go," said Hassan.

Maya, Kaiyo, Beka and Mr Cameraman followed Josie and Hassan out. It was a clear, moonlit evening and the air vibrated with excitement. Mr Cameraman hadn't played an instrument for a long time and, on hearing the varying musical sounds, looked around to find something to make music with.

"Here you go," said Hassan, handing him a small guitar-like instrument, "you might like to play this one."

"Wow!" he said. "That's exactly what I'd like to play!"

Hassan beckoned him to follow and joined in with seven other musicians who were already sitting together, tuning their instruments. Hassan started to play the flute-like instrument, which he had chosen to call a *qualaho*. He felt it made a round calling sound. Josie chose an instrument that looked like a very small harp and played like a violin. "Let's call that one a *lyricio*," said Hassan, as soon as she picked it up.

"That's exactly what it is," said Josie and thought: *He's just like his mother.*

Before long, the cacophony of sounds settled into harmonies, and people were soon humming along. Some started to sing and Hassan loved that the music had brought out their voices. A woman at the back of the crowd came forward; she placed her right hand on her heart and her left on her left ear and sang. She sang in a language that seemed unfamiliar to many, yet everyone was spellbound as if they had understood every word. When she finished, many had their right hand on their heart and tears in their eyes. The woman smiled and sat down, feeling as if she had said everything she needed to say, and that everyone had listened.

After a few seconds Hassan stood up and asked everyone to stand. He asked each person to close their eyes and place their hands exactly as the woman who had just sung had done. They all did and the woman smiled and nodded in appreciation. Hassan then asked them to hum and, as soon as they felt their hum resonating inside, to open their eyes. As people closed their eyes and hummed, they felt their hearts expand and reach out to everyone around them. By the time they had opened their eyes, they felt as if they had reached out to everyone in the whole world. Everyone.

People sat around afterwards long into the night, exchanging stories, feelings and images. The musical instruments had long been put down, and yet music played on in their hearts and in the hum of their voices.

The next morning, the camp was calm and quiet, long after everyone had woken up. People smiled and spoke without words, which reminded Maya of Ramla. She felt that one day she would be there again, although she had no idea when. She was happy to have found her mother, and yet felt that her journey was not complete. She looked at Kaiyo, who seemed to feel the same.

Kaiyo and Maya went to find Josie and Hassan. They had been up for a while, had breakfast and gone for a walk. As Kaiyo and Maya made their way up to the field where Josie and Maya had picnicked on that first morning, they could see it shining brightly in the morning sun.

"It's as if the flowers will never end," said Maya.

"They are beautiful," Kaiyo replied, "and I can see now why yellow was your favourite colour."

Maya put her finger to her mouth to indicate to Kaiyo to be quiet. "I can hear them just over there," she whispered, pointing to the right, and they both sat down in a clearing close by. They knew that Josie and Hassan would join them when they were ready.

Hassan and Josie had become very close; when they came to join Maya and Kaiyo, Hassan sat on Josie's lap. Josie held him close to her and then reached out to Maya and Kaiyo, who knelt down on either side of them and hugged them. Their feelings and thoughts connected and they each knew, with deep silent words, that their journeys were yet to be completed.

Josie placed a hand on Maya's shoulder to let her know that it was okay and that she would always love her. Maya placed a hand on Hassan's head and let him know that he was always free to choose, even when there seemed to be only one choice. He was sure and he had chosen. It was settled, and they would set off at first light the next day. Hassan was the first to make a move; he kissed Josie and asked her if it was okay to spend the rest of the day with her. Josie let him know that she needed to speak to Beka first and then he was free to do just that. They got up and meandered back through the field.

When Josie got back, she found Beka packing and wondered for a second where she was going. With Mr Cameraman, perhaps?

"Going anywhere exciting?" she asked.

"Yes, with you. Along with a few others who'd like to join us. They've started packing too."

"A few others?" replied Josie. "Okay, I'll start packing, then."

It certainly wasn't the first time Josie had led a group of travellers, and this time she wasn't looking for anyone, or going anywhere in particular. She went back to her room to pack and to reconnect with Hassan. She had learnt a great deal from him about reaching out to and connecting with people, and she wanted to let him know. She went first to her box of musical instruments and, as she opened it, she remembered making each and every one. She took a deep breath. *Perhaps Hassan would like to have them*, she thought. She reached for the door handle and opened it, just as Hassan was about to knock on the door. She saw his face and smiled.

"I'll take care of them until we see you next, Josie," he said.

"I know you will, Hassan, just like you take care of everyone and everything around you. You have a way of reaching people that's quite extraordinary to witness. Thank you for sharing it."

He smiled. "I learnt from Mum and Dad."

"You learnt well, Hassan, and I have learnt from you."

Hassan helped Josie to pack and together they went round talking to people around the camp. Everyone was pleased to see them and thanked them for a great night of music the night before. Many commented how light they had felt as they slept and how well they felt now. Those who were staying wished them well on their journeys and those who were intending to travel the next day were glad of their help to pack and prepare.

Everyone chose to get to sleep early that night, to make sure that those who were leaving early the next morning slept well. Maya, as often happened before a big journey, dreamt a beautiful and prophetic dream. Her dream was about her desert princess, the one about whom she had created a story when she was on her way across the desert to the Wadi all those years ago. She saw her riding in the pale morning light, like a shadow in a dark garment that Maya came to know as an *abaya*. It fluttered and billowed in the breeze, held by a rope belt tied around her waist. The belt shone in the sun, as if it were made of gold. At the end of her belt, Maya could see an amulet with two shapes engraved on it that she recognised as letters from another language. They were two Arabic letters, *meem* and *kaef*, the equivalent of the letters M and K.

The princess in her dream came to a pinkish rocky outcrop and brought her horse to a stop. She dismounted with one flick of her whole body and patted her horse in appreciation. She took the amulet off her belt and crouched down to place it gently on the ground. Then she looked up, straight at Maya, and took something from one of her pockets. She opened her hand and blew gently into it to reveal three other amulets, which she placed around the first one. Each had a letter inscribed on it. The first had the letter *hah* (or H), the second had the letter *lam* (or L) and the last had the letter *alef* (or A). The princess then cupped her hands together and placed them over all four amulets for a few seconds, as if protecting them. She looked up at Maya again and smiled, then stood up and turned to her horse. She patted and stroked him in readiness to remount and continue her journey. Before she did so, though, she untied her belt in order to wrap it anew around her waist and, as she did so, the breeze caught her *abaya* and revealed a beautiful, silky, pale yellow gown. The gown was woven and embroidered with a golden silky thread that shone, like the belt, in the sun. The princess closed her *abaya* again, retied her belt and climbed up on her horse, then looked at Maya and beckoned her to follow.

The next morning the camp was vibrant, as those who were travelling prepared to leave. Some were travelling with Josie, Beka and Mr Cameraman; others had chosen to take the opportunity to travel elsewhere. All agreed to make the first part of their journey together to the airfield, then go their chosen way from there. Those who were staying were packing too; packing away things that they felt had weighed them down. No more investigations, no more classifications, no more reporting – just being. Being with themselves and each other, being with the sun and the sky, being with the land and all its bounties, accepting things as they are.

When the travelling group was ready to go, everyone gathered at the edge of the camp to see them off.

"This is it!" shouted Josie at the top of her voice and tossed her hat in the air. "This is the day."

Josie's hat landed next to the woman who had stood up to sing the night before. She picked it up, dusted it off and walked up to Josie. She smiled as she handed it back to her. "We'll be just fine, Josie. You go," she said, "go with all our love and appreciation."

Everyone waved them off. Maya looked at Josie as they climbed into the back of the jeep; she looked full of life. Maya realised in that moment that she'd had some expectations of how her mother would be. She smiled in acknowledgement and let that go. Josie was a great leader, intent on continuing the peace that the Waters had been the cause of, and Maya loved her for it.

As they sat down, Hassan chose to sit next to Josie, and Maya also realised that she'd had expectations of them being together in the next part of her journey. She smiled and let that go too. She turned to look at the Wadi and knew that it would always have a special place in her heart. The softness of the yellow sand mingled with the new savannah, the brilliance of the sun and the warmth of the sun-kissed mountains. She closed her eyes and imagined herself on a horse; she felt the soft pounding of its hooves against the sand and leant in and felt the warmth of its breath, then galloped off into the sun. When she opened her eyes, she saw her desert princess riding beside them with her *abaya* billowing and fluttering in the breeze. As she rode by, she turned to Maya and, as she had done in her dream, beckoned her to follow. At that moment, Maya knew that the next part of her journey was to be on land and, as always, she trusted her instincts to lead her to exactly where she needed to be.

The short journey across the desert to the airport was a significant one. Hassan had changed seats and fallen asleep with his head leaning on Kaiyo's arm. Maya looked at Hassan and smiled and Kaiyo smiled back at her and nodded to let her know that he knew about the next part of their journey too.

Maya had never chosen to journey by land before, at least not since the Waters. She remembered her journey to the Wadi with her mother and Hassan, the guide and driver, all that time ago. She somehow felt just the same, as if she was back in the jeep with her mother after looking around the Wadi. It was as if the Waters had never been and nothing had changed; and yet everything was different.

The Earth's healing process had begun with the floods, and many had felt their effect deeply. The healing was now to continue and Maya was present to this and everyone's part in it. It was something of a miracle that had begun in the guise of the Waters. Maya closed her eyes and breathed a deep breath and felt deeply connected within. Suddenly, she knew the significance of the amulets that the desert princess had brought her, and the letters on them. When Maya opened her eyes she smiled and put her hand just below her stomach. *That explains it*, she thought and looked at Kaiyo, who smiled back at her. She felt that he knew too.

When they arrived at the airfield, everyone was silent. Mr Cameraman and Beka got out and opened the doors at the back of the jeep. They stood opposite each other and made a sweeping bow, inviting them to climb out. Josie smiled and picked up her belongings, ready to climb out. Hassan wanted to go first and jumped out, making a star shape with his arms and legs. He turned and looked at everyone else and smiled, as if daring them to do the same. Maya handed him his bag and followed suit, laughing, and turned to the others. Kaiyo handed Maya her bag and jumped out, while beating his chest and making funny noises. Hassan was in stitches of laughter. Kaiyo reached into the back of the jeep for his bag and stood out of the way of Josie, who jumped out in a graceful balletic leap, and everybody clapped. By the time they had all jumped out of the back of the jeep, everyone's mood was lifted.

"Right," said Josie, "we'd better sort out a flight plan to get us all closer to our destinations."

"No need," said Kaiyo. "We have an alternative mode of transport planned."

"Okay," replied Josie, slightly bemused. "And what mode might that be, Captain, since there are no boats here?" she asked, turning round to demonstrate this … and there they were.

"Wow," said Hassan. "Are those for us?"

There were four camels being led by a man in full Arab dress. "I see," Josie said, smiling. "A ship of the desert, that's the way to travel around here."

Hassan was excited at seeing a new animal and the idea of riding on it. He gave Josie a big kiss and a hug goodbye. "See you soon," he said.

"That's my intention," replied Josie. "I have a few people to meet and a few things to do on the way first, so it may be a while before we meet again."

"Okay," he said, smiling.

Hassan turned to pick up the box of musical instruments.

"I will help you," said the man holding the camels as Hassan noticed his deep brown eyes. The man gestured to Kaiyo to hold the camels' ropes loosely.

"Thank you," he said, as he secured the box on the back of Hassan's camel. He smiled at Hassan, "It will be safe," he said.

Hassan looked at the camel. "Just relax," said the man as he smiled and handed Hassan some clothes.

"First you need to put these on to protect you from the sun and the sand." Hassan looked at the clothes, a long gown and a cloak and a cloth. He was not quite sure what to do with them. The man showed Hassan how to put them on. First the *kaftan*, the long gown, then the *kaffiyeh*, the cloth to go on his head and cover his mouth and nose, and finally the *abaya*, the cloak to go over the top.

"Like this," said the man, as he showed Hassan how to put the *kaffiyeh* on and secure it round his head. "Good?" he asked, and Hassan nodded.

The man with the deep brown eyes then gave a gentle downward tug on one of the camel's reins, and the camel knelt down. Hassan looked at its long eyelashes and smiled as he climbed into the saddle and relaxed, just as the man had suggested.

Maya turned to Josie. "Mum, we're looking forward to hearing all about your journey when we see you. I'm sorry that we're not coming with you."

Josie smiled. "Darling Maya, you have your own journey to take before we meet again, and I'm looking forward to seeing you all in good time. I love you." Maya and Josie were hugging as Kaiyo approached.

"Darling Kaiyo," said Josie as Maya released her, with some reluctance, "it's just the most amazing feeling to have a son as well and I can't wait to hear the story of your journey too. I love you."

Kaiyo smiled and touched his heart then held Josie's hand with both his. "I love you too, Josie."

"I love you too, Josie!" shouted Hassan.

"And I love you, Hassan darling!" Josie shouted back.

Hassan looked completely at home on the camel with his *kaftan*, *kaffiyeh* and *abaya*, and looked on as Maya and Kaiyo were given theirs. They both put them on as if they knew exactly what to do and, as the other camels knelt down, they climbed into their saddles.

Kaiyo looked at Hassan. "You look relaxed there, Hassan."

"I am," he replied. "And I think I'm going to enjoy riding this camel."

"So am I," replied Kaiyo. "Well, this one anyway."

The man with the deep brown eyes asked them to hold on to the reins and stay relaxed while the camels got up. "It's strange first time. You will get used to it. Just stay relaxed as the camels move." Then he made a forwards and backwards movement as if to show them how. "All the time move as the camels move."

The man then climbed into his saddle and almost immediately all the camels got up. "Whoa," said Hassan as his camel lurched forward, bringing up its hind legs, then jolted backwards to bring up its front legs.

"Move as the camels move," said Maya, smiling, and Hassan relaxed again.

"Okay, ready to go?" asked the man.

"Yes, we are," replied Hassan and off they went.

After everyone had waved their goodbyes, Josie blew a kiss in the direction of the camels. "Go in peace," she said. "Until we meet again, go in peace, Maya, Hassan and Kaiyo."

Josie then turned to the others. "Peace," she said. "Peace. That's all anyone ever wants deep down inside, a place of calm. Otherwise there can be no peace on the outside or on this Earth." Josie knelt down and touched the earth, then looked up to the sky and closed her eyes. "Let there be peace in our hearts today and every day so that we can be at peace from the inside out, in all our lifetimes and beyond."

Hassan looked completely at home on the camel

# CHAPTER TEN

# The Desert Princess

Maya felt a little odd after the camel ride. They had ridden south-west for three, maybe four, hours and the movement of the camel had almost rocked her to sleep. The man with the deep brown eyes had brought them to a little encampment by a group of tall palm trees. He seemed to know some of the people there and they were invited to take food and shelter for the night. They were all happy to accept, and Maya, in particular, was glad of the rest.

After taking a little nap and freshening up, Maya, Kaiyo and Hassan came out of their shelter to find everyone by the fire, ready to eat. They had been waiting for them and, as they approached, they were shown to a place that had been laid out with mats on the ground especially for them. As they sat down they were handed a plate full of all kinds of fruits and vegetables. This was followed by a plate each of a rice dish. There was a silent hum as everyone ate and exchanged the occasional word, mostly about how good the food tasted.

Maya looked into the fire as she ate her last mouthful of rice. *That was lovely*, she thought. *I'd happily eat the same all over again.*

"Eat, please," said the woman who had cooked it, as she handed her more. "Good for you now."

Maya was very grateful; she smiled and accepted happily. The dish was made of short-grain rice and brown and yellow beans, all mixed together with a new type of berry that was very slightly sour; it was delicious. She finished eating and thought she might go for a little walk before going to bed, as she was still feeling very sleepy. The moon was high in the sky and, although it was only a little more than half full, it was very bright.

"*Amar*," said the woman.

"What a beautiful name," said Maya. "Is it your name?"

The woman smiled and shook her head. "It is this," she replied and pointed to the moon.

Maya looked up at the moon and smiled. "How beautiful it is," she said. "And how amazing that we are here in this very place, eating this very food and sharing this very beautiful moon. Thank you."

The woman nodded in appreciation.

"Would anyone like to come for a walk with me before I fall asleep?" asked Maya, and Kaiyo and Hassan sprang to their feet, then looked at each other and laughed. Hassan rushed to his mother's side and linked arms with her.

"What a handsome young man," she said as Kaiyo also caught up with them. "Both of you, that is."

It was a short walk, as both Maya and Kaiyo were happy to get back soon and sleep. Hassan, though, seemed wide awake and was looking forward to playing a little music on one of Josie's instruments. "Is it okay if I play while you're falling asleep?"

"Of course," said Kaiyo, as they got ready for bed. "Just a few minutes though."

Maya nodded even though she was almost asleep and said, "Yes please."

Their beds were made of lightweight rolled-out mats laid crossways, one on top of the other. There was a thick quilt on top that acted as a mattress and another quilt as a cover. Maya snuggled in next to Kaiyo, who wriggled slightly to give her a comfortable place under his arms to put her head. Hassan started playing. His music wafted over Maya's body and Kaiyo felt her relax. He too closed his eyes and let the music envelop him. He breathed in deeply, allowing his nostrils to open wide and feel the beautiful warmth all around them. He gently rubbed his cheek against Maya's hair and fell into a glorious sleep.

The next morning everything was calm. Many travellers had already set out on their journeys and Kaiyo and Hassan left Maya to sleep longer. The man with the deep brown eyes was sitting on the ground sipping a hot drink. He got up to greet them as they approached. He had been chatting quietly to the woman who had cooked last night. Kaiyo noticed a similarity in their looks. "She is my sister," the man said and smiled.

Kaiyo nodded. "Hello," he said to the woman.

She smiled in acknowledgement. "Maya is good?" she asked.

"Yes, thank you. She just needs to rest."

"I make her special drink," she said. "And something to eat for you."

"Thank you," replied Hassan and Kaiyo in unison.

"Please sit," she gestured to the mats on the ground and looked at Hassan. "You make beautiful music from your heart."

Hassan smiled. "Thank you." He loved to connect with people and he felt totally at home here with the camels, the sand, the new vegetation and the expansive sky. He could still see the moon faintly in the sky and feel the warmth of the sun on his back. He let it seep into his skin and through to his bones and felt as if he had the sun inside him.

A few minutes later, Maya came out of the shelter looking serene. "What is that beautiful smell?"

The woman approached her with a large bowl full of a drink that smelt of all the energy of the sun and all its flowers. "Wow," said Maya. "For me?"

The woman nodded. "For you," and handed her the bowl.

Maya looked at the bowl and could see that it had a slight impression on its rim to make it easy to drink from. It had two other impressions, one on either side, to make it easy to hold. She cupped it in her hands and put it to her mouth and almost instantly felt a sense of well-being and wholeness.

She closed her eyes to take her first sip and realised something about the princess's message in her dream. "That's what the princess meant," she said, as she opened her eyes again. "Two. That's who the other two amulets are for."

Kaiyo looked at Maya, "Two!"

Maya nodded and breathed deeply. "Two."

Kaiyo smiled and stroked her face very gently as she continued to drink.

"This morning we will travel a short way," said the man with the deep brown eyes, as Maya sat down. "Only two hours."

"Are we riding the camels?" asked Hassan and went to sit down by Maya.

"We are," replied the man. "You like them?"

"Yes," said Hassan and leant his head on his mother's shoulder.

"Are you ready for this?" she asked. "Two."

"I am, Mum," he said.

After eating a plate full of fruit, followed by a warm cereal broth, they gathered their belongings. They put on their *abayas* and *kaffiyehs* and, now being familiar with the camels, easily climbed into their saddles. Maya felt her camel rise with care and a serene smoothness and as she looked at the horizon, she was also looking forward to meeting her desert princess.

Once more, the man with the deep brown eyes got into his saddle and led the way. He looked back at Maya, Kaiyo and Hassan, who nodded, indicating that they were ready.

The camels set off with a silent ease that marked the rest of their journey. The new desert unfolded with its pockets of new lush meadows, full of yellows and blues, reflecting the sun and the sky. The occasional oranges and reds created a sublime, clarifying contrast. The horizon spread out in all directions, laying out the earth before them. It was as if everything was being created that very second for them to experience.

Two hours later, they could make out the low perimeter wall of an old encampment. It was a warm, earthy pink colour, like the desert mountains that Maya had seen in her dream.

"Ooh, a princess's castle," said Maya.

"Like a dream," said Kaiyo.

A pair of enormous, old, hand-carved wooden doors swung open as they approached, and the man with the deep brown eyes led them in. Maya could hardly believe her eyes when, out of the shadow of the sun, walked her desert princess.

"*Asalamu alaikum*. Peace be upon you," she said. "Welcome," as the camels knelt to let their riders down.

She took Maya's hand, helping her out of her saddle, "*Asalamu alaikum* and welcome to your home, Maya," she said and turned to help.

"You are all most welcome," she said as she gestured to them to join Maya. Then the princess took off an amulet that was attached to her belt; it was hung on a simple, beautifully braided ribbon and inscribed with the Arabic letters *meem* and *kaef*.

She gestured to Maya to open out her palm and placed the amulet flat against it, pressing on it gently. "*Meem* for Maya and *kaef* for Kaiyo," she said and looked at Kaiyo and smiled.

Maya placed it against her heart, then handed it to Kaiyo and the princess gestured to him to wear it. The princess turned to Maya and took out of her pocket a second amulet; this one hung on hand-woven ribbon and was inscribed with the Arabic letter *heh*.

"*Heh* for Hassan," she said, as she placed it in Maya's right palm and smiled at Hassan. Maya placed it against her heart, as she did with the first amulet, then handed it to Hassan, who put it on.

The princess put her hand in a second pocket and brought out two amulets that were each hung on a strip of embroidered cloth. Maya opened both her palms as the princess placed one in each. The first was inscribed with the Arabic letter *lam* and the second with the letter *alef*. "For the two that are to join you together," she said.

"Yes," Maya replied. "Lamya and Amar."

The princess nodded. "Then your journey here will be complete."

Maya placed both amulets against her heart. Kaiyo picked up Hassan with one arm and put the other around Maya.

The princess smiled. "When we are truly together here," she said, pointing to her heart, "we are as one and the world is free and clear."

Maya closed her eyes and felt weightless, timeless and limitless. She saw the Earth as if from above, and saw herself hugging it and melting into it.

She woke up to find herself in a bed surrounded by fine netting gently fluttering in the breeze. She was in a room that had beautiful murals all the way around the walls. She went to get up to look at them and noticed she was wearing a pale yellow, silky gown. On the bed there was a robe of slightly heavier material of the same colour, woven and embroidered with a fine golden thread. She slipped it on and rearranged her hair around it and, as she turned to put her feet down, they slipped directly into a pair of silky golden slippers.

Maya smiled. "Just like a princess," she said.

The walls were covered with a soft plaster and painted in a warm white. The murals were clear to see, although their soft colours seemed to melt into the warmth of the white in the background. The room was rectangular. She walked past a slightly open pair of wooden doors and caught a glimpse of an internal courtyard with a sunken pool and a citrus garden. *I'll come back to you later*, she thought as she breathed in the fresh smell. *First, the murals.* To the right of the doors, the first mural depicted a young girl lying on her front, on her bed, drawing. Her legs were bent up at the knees behind her and crossed at the ankles. In the background Maya could make out a faint outline of a man sitting in a chair. Maya knew that the little girl was her and the man was her father. *He's been watching over me all this time*, she thought.

In the next mural, she was a little older and was sitting up in bed with her mother, looking at a book. *That's when I found out about Kiriyu.*

Maya walked on to the third mural and could see that she was in the Wadi, underwater. There was a skeleton floating near her and what looked like Kaiyo in the background. *Kiriyu?* she wondered. *And Kaiyo?*

In the fourth mural, there was a boat and Maya was lying inside it looking as if she was asleep. Kaiyo was holding the side of the boat with one hand and with his free arm was swimming towards the shore. At the shore, however, she could also see his outline standing with his legs astride and his arms open wide. *He saved me? And yet somehow he was waiting for me.*

The fifth mural was of what looked like her shelter on Ramla, with a circle of people around it. Angel and Faye were clear to see. Maya smiled. *I love that place.*

As she came to the next mural, she recognised herself with a rounded tummy. "Hassan," she whispered. "My angel." And all around her were the children playing on the beach at Healing Waters.

In the seventh mural was the bay at Whispering Winds and one of Kaiyo's boats in the background. *He built beautiful boats; they loved the water and the water loved them.* She could also see Mary at the top of the hill, smiling and waving.

The next painting was of her, Kaiyo and Hassan on the boat sailing towards land with the wind in their hair and broad smiles on their faces. The ninth and last mural was of the Wadi with Josie and Hassan playing their instruments along with the others, surrounded by many people.

Maya smiled as she saw one final place on the wall. "Waiting to be painted," she said as she opened the wooden doors.

The courtyard was surrounded by arches with a covered walkway all the way round. Maya could see that there were several other doors that opened onto the walkway and looked out at the courtyard, and that they were all closed. The sunken pool in the centre had four channels bringing fresh water into it from each side. There were four flowerbeds in between the water channels, planted with citrus trees. The ones closer to the pool were in blossom and the ones further out were bearing fruit.

At two ends of the pool were semicircular steps leading down into it. Maya breathed in the soft heavenly scent of the blossoms, some of which had fallen into the pool. She looked into the water as she slipped off her golden slippers. *Fit for a princess*, she thought, and stepped down onto the first step.

The water enveloped Maya's feet with a soft, refreshing and reviving coolness which she felt energise her. Sensing that no one was around, she slipped off her robe and walked down the soft stone steps into the water. She smiled as she heard the water lapping against her legs and felt the slight tugging of her wet gown around her. As her feet touched the bottom, it felt soft and yielding, almost as if she was making imprints in it as she walked. She moved towards the centre of the pool, and felt as if she was being washed by gentle hands.

Maya floated on her back and allowed the water to support her. She thought of Kiriyu and Kaiyo and Ramla; she knew now that Kaiyo had saved her. She felt a deep sense of peace, and felt

Fit for a princess

complete with her past. She was now present to the two new beings that were at home in her body.

Hassan knocked gently at the door. Maya had been there for two, maybe three hours, and was now in the bathroom drying herself. He and Kaiyo had been helping to prepare the fire and the food and it was time to eat. He came in, all excited, to let her know, and saw the murals on the wall.

He stopped to look at them as Maya walked back into the room wearing a new *kaftan*. "What do you think, sweetheart?" she asked.

"There's a space left over there, Mum."

"I meant about the *kaftan*," she said as she laid her damp gown on the back of a chair.

"It looks nice on you, Mum. You look like the princess." He pointed at the wall, "There's space there for another painting."

"Yes, there is." She sat on the edge of the bed and gestured to him to sit next to her.

"You will always be my first special present," she said and reached for his left hand. She placed it gently on her tummy. "Soon we will feel them moving, and it's just the most amazing thing."

Hassan kept his hand very still, then thought he felt something. "I think I felt them, Mum."

"Did you, darling? That's amazing. It's so magical."

Hassan turned to look at his mother. "Mum, I know that you'll be spending a lot of time looking after Lamya and Amar. Dad told me."

She smiled. "He did? What else did he tell you?"

"It will take a while. I mean, it won't be tomorrow or anything," he said.

"That's true."

"After they come, I will help you, because I'm all grown up now."

"Did Daddy tell you that?" she asked.

"I told myself," he said and suddenly remembered. "I helped make the fire and the food, Mum. Please come to eat; it's ready."

"Thank you, sweetheart. I will."

"Time to eat," Kaiyo said as he breezed in to the room.

"I just told Mum that," said Hassan.

Kaiyo looked at Maya, as if to ask if everything was okay, and she smiled and nodded. "Great," he said. "Let's go and join the others."

"I'll be there very shortly," she replied. She picked up the damp gown and ran her hands over it. *It's beautifully woven,* she thought as she carefully rearranged it on the back of the chair to dry and followed Kaiyo and Hassan out into the main courtyard. It was filled with other travellers who were sitting in circles ready to eat, while others were bringing them food and drink. Maya joined in, handing out food and drink.

"Where did all this come from?" she asked Hassan, who was also helping. Hassan shrugged his shoulders; he wasn't sure.

After making sure that everyone had food, Maya and Hassan finally sat down among a group of people who seemed to be mostly from the desert princess's tribe. She loved that they had created such a welcoming oasis for others to enjoy on their journeys. There was a gentle hum as people ate and exchanged a word or two.

"I don't think I've ever seen so many heads nodding," she said and laughed as she realised that she was doing it too, and suddenly everyone was laughing and nodding.

Maya, Kaiyo and Hassan had come to a real oasis that was fed by natural springs. It had been an oasis for travellers for thousands of years, and especially so after the floods. The oasis, which was known as El Raha, meaning 'The Rest', now had many new plants and fruits growing plentifully and provided well for everyone.

In the few months that Maya, Kaiyo and Hassan were in El Raha, they observed and felt the transformation taking place inside people's hearts. The travellers who passed through brought them news of a world that was waking up to new ways of being. As they helped prepare the fire and food daily and grow and tend new plants, Maya felt that by the time Lamya and Amar were ready to join this world, the world would be ready for them.

On the day they were born, Maya woke up early ready to paint the tenth mural. Before she opened her eyes, she knew that this would be the day. She swung her legs gently over the edge of the bed and put on her golden gown and slippers. She had an image clear in her heart and picked up her brushes to prepare.

Kaiyo woke up to help. "Good morning, my darling," he said. "Is it today?" and Maya nodded.

Kaiyo slipped on an *abaya* over his bed clothes, then put on his slippers and went to bring Maya some water to mix the paints with. As he stepped out into the courtyard, he noticed the faint glow of a new moon disappearing into the morning light. *Amar*, indeed, he thought as he smiled and filled a ceramic pot with water. He came back in to find Maya kneeling and drawing the outline of the painting with a piece of soft, warm earthy-pink stone.

"I love this colour," she said. "I see it a lot in my dreams, and it feels to me like it has all the warmth of the sun inside it." She held the stone for a moment in both her hands as if to warm it. Kaiyo mixed the powder with the water and handed the pot to her.

"Lamya is first," Maya said, as she mixed the paint, "and she is very like Hassan." She paused. "And Amar is just like you, darling."

Two hours later, just as Hassan walked in to hand his mother some fruit and cereal for breakfast, the mural was finished. Maya stepped back. "Thank you, sweetheart! What do you think?"

Hassan walked forward to take a closer look. "Is that me holding Lamya?" he asked, pleased to be in the painting.

"Absolutely, sweetheart. You and she are like two peas in a pod, except you're a very big pea," she said, smiling.

"What's Amar holding in her hand?"

"Is my painting that bad?" asked Maya jokingly.

"It's a pen and a … I'm not sure," he said.

"You will know soon enough," she replied, as she felt a contraction. Hassan placed his hand on his mother's lower back.

"That's just the spot," she said, as she stood up carefully and made her way to the bed. He propped up some cushions for her as she sat on the bed and leant back on them. She slipped off her slippers and swung her legs up onto the bed.

"Please bring the fruit over here for me, Hassan, and come and sit beside me." Hassan did as he was requested.

"Mum?" he said, looking at his mother.

"Not yet, sweetheart," Maya replied before he could complete his question.

When eventually it was time, Lamya was the first to come. She was silent at first, then, as Kaiyo helped her clear her lungs, she cried with the same gusto that Hassan had when he was born to let everyone know that she had joined this world.

Kaiyo laughed. "Okay!" he said. "Okay!" and he cleaned her quickly and placed her on Maya's right side. Maya turned gently towards her.

"Hello, my little darling, Lamya," she said and looked around for Hassan. He was awe-struck as he walked over with a swaddling blanket to put around her.

"Just wait till you see your brother – here he is with a blanket," Maya said to her, and Lamya cried even louder.

Hassan stood motionless as he watched Lamya nuzzle up to her mother and fall silent as she started to feed from her mother's breast. Amar was in no hurry to come out.

"Time to come out, please, Amar," said Kaiyo. "We need one more little push, Maya."

Out came Amar's head with lots of dark silky hair.

"Wow," said both Hassan and Kaiyo at the same time, and then her little body followed.

"Phew, that was easy," said Maya, pushing her hair back from her sweaty brow.

They all laughed and suddenly Amar gave a belch and started crying at the top of her lungs. Kaiyo cleaned and swaddled her and put her down on Maya's left side.

"There," he said, "a complete set."

Maya sighed a grateful sigh. "Complete," she said and smiled serenely. Maya was indeed complete; she was a desert princess as she lay with Lamya and Amar on either side of her and Hassan and Kaiyo on either side of them.

"I am surrounded by angels," she said, "and I am in Heaven. A Heaven on Earth."

# Further Reading and Reference Sources

## *BASILOSAURUS ISIS*

Kiriyu is based on a giant prehistoric whale-like marine mammal known as *Basilosaurus isis*. Fossils were first found in the USA, then later in Pakistan and Egypt. It was initially thought to be a reptile, hence the name *Basilosaurus*, which means King Lizard. It had a very elongated body compared to modern whales and – very unusually – hind limbs. These limbs were very small and unlikely to have been able to support its full weight, although initially they were thought to hark back to an ancestral ability to walk on land.

Further information can be found in the sources listed below:

- *National Geographic* "Whale Found in Egypt Desert" Top 10 News Photos 2005
  *See:* http://news.nationalgeographic.com/news/2005/12/photogalleries/top_ten_pictures/

- *BBC "Basilosaurus"*
  *See:* http://www.bbc.co.uk/nature/life/Basilosaurus

- *Wikipedia "Basilosaurus"*
  *See:* http://en.wikipedia.org/wiki/Basilosaurus

# WADI EL-HITAN

Wadi El-Hitan, or Valley of the Whales, is the area in Egypt where *Basilosaurus isis* fossils were found. It is approximately 150 km southwest of Cairo, the capital city, and was once the ocean bed of an ancient sea, called the Tethys Sea. This ancient sea extended much further south than the Mediterranean Sea and, as it retreated, it left rich sediment and a wealth of marine and plant fossils that can still be seen there today. It was discovered in the winter of 1902 and 1903. Despite being the largest area in the world to have so many well-preserved fossils, it wasn't until the 1980s that interest in it grew. This was largely due to the availability of four-wheel drive vehicles that made the area more accessible. Initially, many bones were removed, leading to calls for its protection and its eventual status as a UNESCO World Heritage site in 2005.

Further information can be found in the sources listed below:

- *The Encyclopedia of Earth* website "Wadi Al-Hitan (Whale Valley)" *See:* http://www.cocarth.org/article/Wadi_Al-Hitan_%28Whale_Valley%29,_Egypt

- *World Heritage Site Image House* "Hitan"
  *See* : http://www.egyptcd.com/eco_Hitan.html

- *Wikipedia* "Wadi Al-Hitan"
  *See:* http://en.wikipedia.org/wiki/Wadi_Al-Hitan

- *UNESCO World Heritage List* "Wadi Al-Hitan (Whale Valley)"
  *See:* http://whc.unesco.org/en/list/1186

- *Encyclopaedia Britannica* "Tethys Sea" by Carol Marie Tang
  *See:* http://www.britannica.com/EBchecked/topic/588887/Tethys-Sea

# INDIAN OCEAN TSUNAMI

The Indian Ocean tsunami of 2004 was certainly the most deadly and arguably the most devastating ever recorded. It was reported by the US Geological Survey (USGS) to have unleashed energy equivalent to 23,000 Hiroshima-type atomic bombs. It killed 150,000 people on the first day and 230,000 in total, leaving many more missing and homeless. Eleven countries around the Indian Ocean were affected. The earthquake had the longest duration of faulting ever observed. The entire planet vibrated, triggering earthquakes as far away as Alaska. Notably, the islands of the Maldives were affected by the flooding, yet very few people died there, probably because they were protected from the worst of it by the outlying coral reefs. The protection provided by well maintained reefs, mangroves, sand dunes, and other natural coastal features such as peat swamps, has been observed in previous tsunamis and floods. They help reduce the energy in the waves and provide a natural barrier.

Further information can be found in the sources listed below:

- *National Geographic News* "The Deadliest Tsunami in History?" January 2005
  *See:* http://news.nationalgeographic.com/news/2004/12/1227 _041226_tsunami.html
- *Wikipedia* "2004 Indian Ocean earthquake and tsunami"
  *See:* http://en.wikipedia.org/wiki/2004_Indian_Ocean_ earthquake_and_tsunami
- *Global Development Research Centre* "The Indian Ocean tsunami and its environmental impacts" by Hari Srinivas
  *See:* http://www.gdrc.org/uem/disasters/disenvi/tsunami.html